Sex of the Stars

MONIQUE PROULX

Sex of the Stars

TRANSLATED BY
MATT COHEN

DOUGLAS & McINTYRE
VANCOUVER / TORONTO

Douglas & McIntyre
1615 Venables Street
Vancouver, B.C. V5L 2H1

The author thanks the Quebec Ministry of Cultural Affairs.

The publisher gratefully acknowledges the assistance of the Canada
Council and of the British Columbia Ministry of Tourism, Small
Business and Culture.

Canadian Cataloguing in Publication Data

Proulx, Monique, 1952-
[Sexe des étoiles. English]
Sex of the stars

Translation of: Le sexe des étoiles.
ISBN 1-55054-495-0

I. Title. II. Title: Sexe des étoiles. English.
PS8581.R6883S413 1996 C843'.54 C95-911226-X
PQ3919.2.P73S413 1996

Cover design by Michael Solomon
Printed and bound in Canada by Metropole Litho Inc.

I who live and die
contemplate you, the stars.
The earth no longer holds
the child she has carried.
Close to the gods
in the night of a hundred veils
my infinitesimal being
joins to your vastness.
And I taste
my share of eternity.

PTOLEMY
(as translated by Marguerite Yourcenar)

ONE

So this was what making others suffer felt like: a kind of boredom, composed of torpor, morosity and a feeble ghost of guilt—the guilt over feeling nothing, in fact—a mixture that was finally benign, and didn't prevent Gaby from appreciating the light's ochre density this autumn noon, or, alas, her stomach from rumbling.

Things were going badly.

The two of them were sitting at the table next to the kitchen window—although "sitting at the table," so far as René was concerned, was a more than dubious euphemism. He was bent over himself, as though his spinal column had been removed, and he was sobbing. That sobbing apparently originated in his pulmonary lobes, rose and scraped through his convulsing diaphragm, continued up his windpipe in asthmatic bursts, then finally exploded, inexhaustible gurgling geysers pouring out from several openings in his head. This had been going on for hours and had lost, it must be said, its initial effect. Just the same, Gaby managed a few apologetic quivers, or at least their appearance. After all, for a long time she had loved this man, with a neurotic immoderation he had never returned, but too bad, it was too late to balance the books. Now was the time to make the break. This had been unilaterally decreed by

Gaby, which complicated the process, even though it had been launched a month ago.

There was a third and not negligible protagonist in the kitchen, the cheese, a perfectly ripe Gorgonzola, coated with a bluish sweat, shimmering and fragrant. This bacterial fermentation was happily juxtaposed with a loaf of crusty bread that Gaby had cut into slices in the hope of using the one with the other, and vice versa. Now this goal, simple though it might have seemed, turned out to be difficult to achieve. You don't eat beside someone who is crying; that is hardly polite, in fact it is most certainly rude and unfeeling. And while René, a living allegory of the ontology of human distress, struggled in the grip of a limitless despair, Gaby looked unhappily at the Gorgonzola and hated herself for being hungry—but what can be done against an empty stomach.

There was a sudden lachrymal lull: once more René's body assumed its usual lanky form, his voice became capable of speech, his eyes almost dry. Gaby stretched her hand out towards the cheese.

"I want to know his name," René belched out.

"Whose name?" Gaby asked stupidly, her hand suspended.

"Don't play the idiot. The guy you're sleeping with."

There was no other man, no one, no exterior motive to blame, nothing but a very ordinary and small death of love, the one that inevitably germinates in the soul of the partner who has been ripped off by the other, "nothing but a very ordinary slave uprising, my love," she had nevertheless explained thirty days before, already.... But he didn't believe her, would never believe her, no one wants a mere truth without the dazzle of sensational infidelities.

"I'll kill him. First him, then you."

And he began crying again, because the senseless things he was saying provided no relief. Meanwhile Bertrand's van, Bertrand being René's younger and very patient brother, was waiting outside, filled with René's meagre personal belongings. For years, in fact, René had been clinging to her possessions and to her like a kind of tapeworm. Bertrand honked timidly. Gaby took advantage of this to sigh. The role of the torturing Gorgon was beginning to weigh on her, in the long term it set up a situation that was redundant, excessively masochistic and vaudevillian in the worst sense. Also, her stomach was now rumbling so loudly it drowned out René's sobs.

"It would be better if you went," she said decisively, exasperated by her hunger, and she took the risk of preparing herself a huge piece of bread and Gorgonzola, her eyes closing in sumptuous anticipation.

That had an unhoped-for effect. For a moment René looked uncomprehendingly at them—her and her bread and her cheese—then he quietly stood up, politely slid his chair back into place, and stood bent over Gaby for a moment as though about to embrace her—a gesture oh so familiar which awoke in her an old tremor of tenderness. She turned her head towards him for a kiss. That was the exact moment he chose to spit in her face, a gob so voluminous that it entirely covered her eyes and part of her left cheek. Then he left the apartment. Gaby listened, petrified, to the sound of the van as it disappeared down the street. After which she wiped her face on the tablecloth and swallowed three-quarters of the Gorgonzola without even bothering to spread it on the bread.

•

She arrived late at CDKP, the city's most amusing radio station, or so it advertised itself. Mrs. Wagner, at the entrance, mummified in her glass cage over her police tabloid, her lower lip quivering with emotion, at the mercy of the blood-soaked tales she was reading, didn't even raise her eyes as Gaby swept by calling out hello—she only greeted the on-air hosts and the managers, who, for their part, showed no more interest in her than in a mule-dropping. So life goes, full of one-way streets and dead ends.

Gaby's guests were waiting for her in the tiny cubbyhole the researchers used as an office, which stank of piss-of-rutting-cat seasoned with springtime-rose-of-Florient, since the latter fragrance, painfully ineffective, was used to try to wipe out the former, with which the previous occupant, to all appearances a ferocious felinophile, had impregnated the very soul of the room's furnishings.

The day's guests were two men, Mr. Nutt and Mr. Joy, both fat but one much more so than the other, with cascading flesh that piled into several spare tires held in place by a single belt.

"Good day," Gaby said, out of breath, "which of you is Mr. Nutt?"

"That's me," said the man with the quadruple abdomen, standing up with amazing speed.

"Excuse me," said the less fat one, whose stomach had only one fold, but a substantial one, "I was first. Joy. William Joy."

He got to his feet, but more slowly than the other man.

"That could be," Nutt said, cracking a smile, "but the lady asked for Nutt. Arthur Nutt."

"I got here an hour before you did, so I've been waiting

for an hour and a half," said Mr. Joy, his chubby face suddenly wrinkling up as though he was going to cry.

"It doesn't matter," Gaby soothed. "Anyway, you'll be on the air in two minutes, both of you."

"Together?" the two men exploded at the same time.

"One after the other. Mr. Mireau will decide the order. Okay, now let's have a quick run-through, we're very late. First, the therapy by...uggh...eating fatty foods."

"That's me," Mr. Nutt warbled. "I brought my book: *Fat and Happy*."

"Big pile of shit," the other sighed, collapsing defeated on his chair.

"I'll sign a copy for you if you like."

"I already have one," Gaby declined. "Give it to Mr. Mireau. For the interview, I want to ask—"

"But I gave him a book, I sent it to him priority post, it cost me ten dollars and eighty-five cents. He didn't get it?"

"I've been waiting an hour and a half," Mr. Joy moaned, spread out on the chair. "My slugs are going to die, for sure."

Gaby, worried, glanced quickly around the room. "Oh yes, the healing slugs. Where...where are they?"

"Healing slugs!" Mr. Nutt burst out laughing. "What can they cure?"

"I didn't ask you anything, blubberpuss," Joy snapped. "They're here. In my pocket. Wrapped up in lettuce, poor little things."

"Maybe they should have a bit of air," Gaby admitted. She was starting to get a headache.

"NO WAY! They don't like daylight."

"Slugs!" Mr. Nutt couldn't get over it. "Jesus on toast, what can they cure?"

"Cancer and venereal diseases," Gaby said. "And speaking of your little mites, during the interview, maybe it would be better—"

"CORONARY diseases!" Mr. Joy corrected haughtily. "And it's none of his business, this big bag of jelly who comes late and then butts in!"

"My goodness, I'm afraid I find you very aggressive," Mr. Nutt deplored with an apologetic smile. "I'll send you one of my books. It will teach you inner peace."

"That's you, inner grease."

"Disgusting slob."

"Fat greaseball quack!"

"Stupid slugbrain!"

The script girl arrived, and led them to the studio before they tore each other apart. In sum, it was a day like other days, off to a running start.

The program was called "Not So Crazy" and racked up an amazing number of listeners; for Gaby it meant exhuming the strangest creatures that could be found from their anonymous hiding-places and bringing them to the CDKP studio, where Bob Mireau, the celebrated host, gave himself the job of destroying them in an amusing way. Some of these guests revealed themselves to be truly insane, with delusions so imaginative that you had to admire them. Most, unfortunately, were just very ordinary crazies, with small and insignificant eccentricities that barely distinguished them from the common herd. In truth, oh sign of the times, Madness, beautiful, silky, crackling madness, was undergoing an irreversible degeneration and was on the road to extinction.

When the taping was finished, and the slug farmer and the obese therapist had been reintegrated into the ranks of the silent multitude, Bob Mireau came to sit beside Gaby, who was carrying on three simultaneous conversations by using three telephones and an avant-garde technique she herself had brought to perfection. He kissed her neck, as always taking advantage of the opportunity to feel up her left breast, while she set down the last receiver.

"It seems to me you're losing a bit of weight, my sweet," he said nicely.

"I'm screwing too much. It eats you up."

"Fat and happy," Bob sighed—proving that he had indeed become acquainted with Mr. Nutt's masterpiece.

He was a superficial and charming man who skimmed life's surface like a water strider—eating, drinking, sleeping with beautiful women, joyously rambling on about futile subjects...and maybe that was the idea after all, Gaby couldn't help telling herself, as she observed him making his way, flourishing and content. They had gone to bed a couple of times, since this was the only way to have any kind of intimacy with him, and Gaby remembered these occasions as easy and inconsequential: he plumbed her with a light and playful touch, all the while telling jokes, and afterwards he didn't snore.

"What sickening little concoctions are you working on?"

"Some choice morsels, my dear. A girl who predicts the future by reading knee joints. A biker who converted to Bahai. Then the next week, a transsexual."

"A transsexual. Yum-yum. Nuts and tits: there's a combination that's always excited me."

"Sorry to disappoint. Just tits. The nuts have been knackered."

Bob Mireau's eyes suddenly grew anxious and cloudy. He contemplated Gaby with a new seriousness.

"You mean the poor bastard really got them cut off?"

"SHE got them cut off. Don't forget to address her as a woman."

"Damn, damn," Bob Mireau muttered as he stood up. "We live in an age filled with horrors."

He was about to return to the studio when Gaby took his hand. "I'm tempted to go to your place this evening," she said, with calculated indifference.

"Impossible, chickie. I already have a date."

"Cancel it."

"Cancel HER, you mean ...."

He raised an eloquent eyebrow towards Priscilla—twenty years old, corkscrew hairdo, mountainous curves, and a typist's contract with CDKP that was about to expire—who had just made her languid and sinuous way across their field of vision.

"Ah," said Gaby, surprised, "so you haven't done it with Priscilla yet?"

"Not yet. I'm a very busy man."

"Too young. She'll be boring in bed."

"Probably. But what a bum! Oh Mammon, oh merciful Astaroth, oh all-powerful Beelzebub! And what amazing bazooms! Have you ever seen such bazooms?"

"Great," Gaby agreed generously. "She must have a gland problem."

Bob Mireau had to be given credit for one thing: since he had become part of Gaby's professional circle, he had made her acquire considerable skill, notably in the casual production of crude and salacious remarks. She who used to redden like an amanita mushroom at the least vulgar of jokes now discussed the tumescence of pricks and the moistening of pussies without even a blink; when she met a man for the first time she looked at him right where it counts, between the legs. She regarded herself as thus better equipped for life than ever—without being able to figure out exactly how.

"Then have a good evening, you pig. And at least use a condom, instead of planting your children in every available hole."

"Tsk, tsk. If I didn't know you so well, I'd say you were jealous."

"Not jealous, frustrated. It's been a dry month, even with myself."

"Bad for the health, Gaby-poo. Incidentally, have you seen my silver pencil? I've been looking for it for an hour, damned mind is going senile...."

"No," said Gaby, turning quickly back to her papers to hide the blush she now felt invading her cheeks.

"Too bad. It was a gift. Another woman who's going to want to kill me....I live dangerously, but that's my life. *Ciao*, chickie."

After kissing the back of her neck, Bob Mireau left. Gaby heard him talking to himself in the corridor, then stopping beside someone, obviously Priscilla, to whisper some inaudible joke. The tiny office had grown dark, but Gaby didn't turn the lights on; this was the time of day for half-colours, blurred edges and, unless you were careful, the sharp beginnings of anxiety. Struck by an unwanted intuition, she looked in her purse; the silver pencil, of course, was there.

It was nine-thirty when Gaby finally slid her two keys into the two indestructible and impregnable triple-pivot locks that guaranteed her and her possessions security against the world's malevolence. She took care to call out, "It's me," to show just how indifferent she was to the fact that no one answered. The apartment was beautiful, clean and as cold as a deserted château. In the air was a faint odour of talc or vegetation.

She put on some music: the odes of Papathanassiou, chanted in the beautiful dramatic voice of Irene Pappas. Afterwards, on television, she watched the moving lips of Bernard Derome, then those of Pierre Nadeau, Simon Durivage, and a quantity of other individuals whose names she didn't know, all of whom seemed eager to tell her something important. She turned off the television. Now the vegetable odour was winding itself around her. She went to the kitchen, threw the liquefied remains of the Gorgonzola into the garbage, opened the windows wide. The smell wavered slightly with the impact of the cold air, then returned in force, as insistent as incense.

Gaby shut herself in the bathroom. There was nothing to be done against the smell, it was that of René and six years of life together, the stubborn odours of rage, madness and love, a small pile of crumbly bones that would inevitably lose their power to evoke. Human passion is so ridiculous. She started to chew at the numerous sleeping pills an obliging druggist had supplied. Suddenly, in the mirror, she saw something that froze her: there was, on the triangular face of the girl staring back at her, an intense desire to live. She spat the sleeping pills into the toilet, went back into the kitchen and, since she was hungry, gulped down three entire bags of vinegar-flavoured potato chips.

TWO

IT was not hunger that was driving the jaws of Dominique Larue. Yes, he was masticating, because, as though by telekinesis, the bloodless remains of the anonymous beast stagnating in the midst of his plate had begun stagnating in his mouth, and it was necessary to get rid of them. It was the dinner hour; the room was filled with a number of masticating mouths that managed simultaneously to emit all sorts of audible words, a feat admirable in itself. No less admirable were the owners of these multitalented jaws, because they belonged to well-known writers assembled in Montreal for an international colloquium. Dominique Larue was invited, and was thus a writer; that is to say, twelve years earlier he had perpetrated a three-hundred-page novel that had been a great success in the eyes of the critics and three thousand two hundred and two readers. Since then he had exuded nothing, *rien*, *nada*, *tipota*, *niente*, not a single line.

In fact he was eating out of fear, in order to keep his teeth from chattering. In a few minutes, as soon as the communal meal was finished and the final cerebral winds had broken, the great minds would transport themselves into a waiting room, more or less preceded by their weighed-down bodies, and there they would await his pronouncements. He had to give a speech, that was the worst thing; he had to prove to all the Goncourt prize-winners that he was one of them. Might as well try to identify with a Precambrian millipede, or a telephone booth. What was more, the meaning of the obligatory theme of his speech—*The function of spasm in writing*—had totally escaped him until now; a bit late, he finally realized that the spasm he should have been talking about was the existential spasm, the seismic earthquakes of psychoconsciousness in the expanded soul of the creator which are set off by the object in the process of being created, at least that was what had been suggested by the Polish authoress who had spoken a few moments before, and she had been loudly applauded, which must prove something.

Since the beginning of the colloquium Dominique had been sagging under the edifying speeches; the edification of the others stunned him and he was rendered as silent as a frozen smelt. He never should have agreed to come, of course, as the man said to himself while being escorted to his place in the electric chair. The responsibility for the error was once again Mado's, it was she who had dramatically begged him, her throat quivering with emotion, not to refuse the honour he was finally being offered, which, moreover, would be his for all eternity. She continued to see him as a Balzacian offshoot, possibly inoculated at birth with genes from Albert Cohen and Réjean Ducharme, a kind of monstrous tricephalic genius who was, it went without saying, devastating yet unknown, while he himself had long ago realized that he was nothing but dried-out sand beside which the Sahara desert could pass for a botanical garden.

Seated at the same table were 1) a bald man with coal-black eyes called Giacomo Luzzi, who had written forty-two novels and fifteen books of essays translated into some twelve languages, all living; 2) a Quebec woman novelist named Violette Bouvier-Paradis, who was published in Paris and couldn't get over not having been born there; 3) a short Yugoslavian man whose name was impossible to pronounce and who worked in the field of neo-epic drama and whose work had twice almost won the Nobel Prize; 4) a short, drooling man named Guillaume Triche who talked non-stop and *had* been born in Paris; 5) an American, Mary Beck, whose incisors were as long as her bibliography; and 6) the ghost of Dominique Larue, white and voiceless, as was proper.

The conversation was about how computerized word-processing systems interfered with the writing process and the literary life: was it necessary to see, on the part of capitalist societies, an odious push towards productivity, an attempt to rehabilitate and transform the Author into a book-excreting machine as had been forecast by Marx in *Capital and the State*, or was the computer really a liberating tool which finally wired the creator directly to his intuitive flashes and spared him the dreary practical contingencies involved in the manual production of words—white-out fluid, typewriter ribbons, even ink for pens and other neanderthal instruments...? That was the question, and it was a tough one. Violette Bouvier-Paradis was of the opinion that Giacomo Luzzi was right, despite the fact that the great literary genius was more inclined to rambling shaggy-dog stories than to defining a clear position; Guillaume Triche lyrically defended modernity as though it were about to become extinct; Mary Beck couldn't get a word in edgewise, so contented herself with ferociously baring her large clacking teeth; the short Yugoslav soliloquized in a low voice, speaking Serbo-Croatian, which made him hard to understand; Dominique opined this way and that, to give the impression of thinking something, or at least of being somewhere.

In fact he found himself sent twenty-five years into the past, into the nervous skin of the little boy he had once been; the phys ed course was drawing to a close and in a few seconds he was going to have to execute, on the pommel horse, that perilous double somersault the others leapt into so eagerly, in a sort of graceful weightlessness, and of which he was totally terrified. He closed his eyes. With all his strength he begged some obscure deity to spare him the plunge to his death, in brief to enact a miracle, and the miracle invariably arrived. The little Tougas boy ahead of him broke his jaw on the trampoline, the ambulance had to be sent for; there was a sudden fire drill and the whole school rushed towards the exit; the teacher suddenly succumbed to a storm of theoretical explanations and the bell rang before it was Dominique's turn....A deity both obscure and compassionate.

"HeyyouwhatdoyouthinkofthatMonsieurLarue," Guillaume Triche said suddenly, looking towards him, and the heads of the others docilely followed the Parisian example and pointed towards Dominique, who instantaneously fell back into his adult skin, twisted with anxiety: what do they want from me, I didn't do anything!—unless it was a question, in which case the horror knew no bounds and the only solution was euthanasia.

It was a question.

"That is to say that," Dominique ventured, "to the extent that everything is relatively known...."

(At this moment a pro-Gadhafi Palestinian brigade clad

in tunics and bulletproof vests appeared in the dining room, their Kalashnikovs smoking in their fists, screaming imprecations in bad French while machine-gunning some Israeli guests disguised as writers; hit by mistake, Guillaume Triche was the first to collapse into the green vegetables, which cut short the question.)

"I think," Dominique continued nonetheless, stoic as a saint in the midst of the terrifying general attention, "I think in the end that I think, ha-ha, in brief, one must try to be, in fact, happy."

A pained silence hung over the table for a few seconds—he obviously hadn't said the right thing—then the beginning of a titillation of interest reached the spinal column of the great Giacomo Luzzi.

"Happy," he sighed intensely. "Happy-happy-happy-happ—"

It seemed that there were, after all, unlikely though it might have first appeared, possibilities within that word, and the debate reignited. Was happiness a Mephistopheleian obstacle to the writer's creativity, destroying the great zones of pain and darkness from which stem, as everyone knows, the precarious rhizomes of neurosis and genius, or rather was the creator, burdened with his mission, the inheritor of a natural and sacred duty he could not set aside, similar in that respect to the least human of beasts and the filthiest garbage collector, to know the moral imperative of trying to achieve happiness?...

Meanwhile, a small background pandemonium: nameless waiters had replaced the uneaten leftovers with other victuals. Dominique found himself cutting up and, with the same bovine impassivity, stuffing down an entire round of Auvergnat blue cheese—it was only after he'd made it disappear from his plate that he remembered that he detested cheese and that, moreover, he had also swallowed the paper wrapping.

(At this moment he collapsed on the floor, victim of an attack of indigestion or something else—whatever might be necessary—and the great minds themselves, shocked and overwhelmed with pity, sent him home special delivery express with words of encouragement and friendly claps on the back.)

Time passed with an obtuse but inevitable slowness. Now that coffee had been served, Dominique Larue drank it by the gallon, thinking that in a few moments he would die of shame, of confusion, of being insignificant, he was going to die and he was terribly alone with the agonizing pain of those who are about to die, o my brothers, my fellows, my non-fellows, he would have given anything, even if at this moment nothing more remained to him, to feel some breath of solicitude around him, to feel that along with all these words so full of cleverness came a little humanity. But people were getting up, the time for coffee was slipping away into the shining black-ice nothingness, he was going to have to stand up like the others, push back his chair a bit to do so, wipe his chops for the last time, with that absorbed look of those who have existential preoccupations or suffer from constipation, and walk, what hell, towards his unnameable fate.

The short Yugoslavian was lingering near the table; Dominique, with the fogged vision of those condemned to death, saw him putting two buns and a saltshaker into his attaché case—times must be hard, even for those eligible for the Nobel. Standing in front of them, Guillaume Triche continued his conversation with Violette Bouvier-Paradis's chest, which his eyes never left, Mary Beck's teeth laughed loudly at a joke no one else understood, Giacomo Luzzi had been snatched up by colleagues from the next table, and all these intelligences advanced, murmuring, towards the exit, glorious bipeds of the nuclear era doomed to extinction, but nobody was thinking about that.

(At this moment a tide of hysteria swept the crowd. Mary Beck, who was no less than an escaped Transylvanian vampire, sank her voracious eyeteeth into the neck of the great Giacomo Luzzi, while Guillaume Triche tried to rape Violette Bouvier-Paradis, who counterattacked with a totally unexpected left hook, sending the crowd into an uproar and causing the definitive suspension of the international writers' colloquium....)

A hand grabbed Dominique's elbow, almost sending him into an apoplectic fit; the depressive smile of Denis Fafouin, philosopher-president of the colloquium, hovered a few inches from his face.

"Just a word, my dear Larue Dominique, concerning your speech...."

It was this moment he should have chosen—had the so-called Larue Dominique still retained even a fragment of rationality—to invoke the terrifying cataclysms, mortalities and diverse pathologies that kept him from putting two coherent sentences together. But he said nothing, allowing himself to be dragged along to the hall like a zombie, Denis Fafouin's hand and voice enclosing him like a high-quality Saran Wrap before leaving him there alone, cornered between the auditorium and the public toilets. He had aged, the obscure and compassionate deity of his childhood no longer seemed inclined to conjure up miracles in his favour.

Nevertheless, beside the auditorium was the word EXIT, printed in red neon above a door, and behind that word EXIT and that double door lay the ever-expanding universe. Thus it was that Dominique Larue, on this sunny end-of-October day, suddenly decided to take his destiny in hand, i.e. to escape, and he passed through the double door that led to freedom and the ever-expanding universe.

Park Avenue had never been so beautiful, full of finely tuned cars roaring and backfiring and spitting out astral clouds of dust and carbon monoxide. He loved the city and its smell of chemical corruption; he loved the policeman who looked at him, in passing and for nothing, with the face of a vindictive brontosaurus; he loved the dog-shit his shoes had just accidentally landed in. Life was good, life was to be greedily savoured and drunk down; once more he was a happy nobody wandering hither and yon with no goal other than to put out his right foot and then his left, that was how men had walked since the beginning of time and they were no worse for it. It was only farther up, at the intersection of Saint Joseph and in this blissful state, that Dominique suddenly saw her. She had just emerged from a connecting street or a restaurant, she had appeared, in fact, as though from nowhere, and there she was, moving away from him swaying and fluid and in a hurry to arrive elsewhere. Dominique thought first of an antelope, purebred and furtive like the ones on television programs about exotic animals; then he thought of a flame; then he said to himself that it was a woman and that she had an amazing way of disappearing from his life. Without even realizing it, he had speeded up. She must have been in her thirties, possibly twenty or fifty, it didn't matter, the truth was that nothing mattered except the timeless vitality that allowed her to move with such distinction through the crowd, an elf among baboons. She wasn't very tall, her wrists and ankles were delicately shaped, her back was curved in a particularly moving way that gave the impression of moaning beneath the black cloth of her coat, and that hair, a sumptuous ochre and mahogany in which the sun was going wild—but in its place who wouldn't have?

But before the sneers and sniggers begin, let it be made clear that Dominique Larue was no lascivious skirt-chaser. In ten years of living with Mado, his girlfriend, he had had only two or three flesh attacks, and those had been at the beginning of their relationship, before the sterile desert had reached so far, extended, it must be admitted, right into his penis. He wasn't unhappy about it, or so he had believed until now; in fact he believed in all sorts of serious things: fidelity, the grandeur of art, the political independence of Quebec; but now, all of a sudden, behind this woman on Park Avenue at the corner of Saint Joseph, he knew that he was dying from an acute lack of life, that he had shrivelled up from his lack of ambition and the vapid emptiness of his life with Mado.

She came to the intersection of Laurier, and Dominique saw that she was going to angle to the left. Into his mind came entire chunks of Baudelaire he hadn't realized he knew:

A flash....Then night!—Fleeting beauty,
In your eyes I am suddenly reborn,
Will I not see you 'til eternity?
Somewhere, so far from here! Too late! Or never!
I do not know your way, nor you mine,
Oh, I might have loved you, and you knew!

She was turning left; he was going right, brutally brought down to earth, back to the apartment and Mado, who would welcome him with their unbearable habitual affability, so that was how this was going to end—this nothing, this congealed little sketch of something that would never happen. He felt a terrible sadness, a panic—this woman who was moving off in her magic would only exist for other men, her black and walnut back fleeing, fleeing with his dreams and pounding heart and life, real life.

He made a sudden and insane decision. He, Dominique Larue, thirty-eight years old, sensible person, dried-up writer, reflective PQ supporter; he started to run after her, knocking over passers-by and laughing. He had become young again, he would tell her incredible things she would have to believe, I have nothing but I'm leaving it all behind, I'm leaving my girlfriend, give me ten days or a hundred or a thousand, surround me in the incredible rush of your beauty, make me vibrate and vibrant, let us commit, yes, let us commit wild deeds so death never catches us....

She turned around, she could only be beautiful, with that incensed look in her eyes, or amused, or already marked by some competing passion....

She turned around. He froze, thunderstruck.

"Oh hi!" said Mado, his girlfriend. "I got my hair dyed. How do you like it?"

THREE

CHENILLE wornheel slipperyeel freefeel camille. Camille. Ugly first name, forced genuflection of the tongue into long vowels that Mme Trotta took pleasure in stretching out endlessly before the class in her nasal accent, as though in order to insult her.

"Camiiiiyyyy...?"

Camille stood up quickly, to cut the teacher off, and went towards the green blackboard, her arms tangled in charts and illustrations which hung to the ground and kept getting underfoot as she walked.

It was French 101, an overpopulated class swarming with monstrous preadolescents. Mme Trotta, who had been a French-speaking Swiss in some far-off past but was now just a frightened and depressive entity, dispensed her flaccid lessons in a state of primal terror. As a token of esteem she had been renamed "Mme Blotto," and with each year the miseries inflicted aged her by ten. But she endured. She must have been immortal. For the moment she was allowed an instant of respite, she was looking at Camille with a kind of joyous malice, *Aha, you wretched creature!* her expression seemed to be signalling, now it's your turn to face the monsters. As for Camille, she wasn't looking at anyone. Serious as an archaeologist, she unfolded her charts and illustrations and stuck them carefully to the board. Wild brayings had begun rising from the class, mixed with various burps and hysterical growls, as though a whole herd of mastodons was pawing and restless, but Mme Blotto hardly blinked, she was reconciled to the worst, and Camille contented herself with delicately clearing her throat and looking outside, in the expectation of some unlikely silence—which nevertheless arrived. The students had just noted the unusual nature of the illustrations covering the blackboard: there was a kind of violently coloured diagram, with enigmatic figures along the X and Y axes, orange-coloured balls and a sinuous sled in the centre; most of all there was a gigantic poster with a black background splotched with intense luminous splashes, about which it was difficult to understand anything except that it was incomprehensible and very beautiful.

"That," Camille took the opportunity to say in her slightly acid voice, "is a Hertzprung-Russell diagram. And this is the constellation Canis Major. I'm going to talk to you about the stars."

So this was giving a speech: a jolt of uncontrollable terror followed by the amazing phenomenon of... POWER. To hold their eyes and the insides of their heads captive, to let her words go forth into the stunned silence of the others, to watch Marineau's flabby mouth trembling with respectful incomprehension, to see the frozen expressions of Sylvie, Grand-Dé, Anemone Bouchard, Richard Leduc, to have the Bouctouche brothers looking at her longingly, to see in the handsome Lucky Poitras's meditative expression a staggeringly delicious, unmistakable beginning of interest. And Camille, who at eleven years old was the youngest in the class, spoke for three minutes into a silence that could have been cut with a knife.

"The stars live and die," she was saying. "Like people. Like trees. When we see a star in the sky it may have been dead for years, but we still see it. There are big stars and little stars. The little stars live longer than the big ones. When a big star dies, it explodes, it becomes a supernova, and we can see it from here. Before that it turns bright red, like Betelgeuse. The small stars don't explode, they turn into white dwarfs, then into black dwarfs, and the black dwarfs, we don't know for sure, but they may be like some kind of street-cleaning machine that sucks up everything around it. I'm going to tell you some star names to show you how beautiful they are: Aldebaran, Alpha Centauri, Denebola, Delta Cephei, Bellatrix, Regulus, Epsilon Aurigae, Pollux, Capella, Castor. This one here is called Sirius; when you look at it in the telescope it always seems to be moving. It's going to die in six million years."

Then Mme Blotto spoke. During this whole time she had been surreptitiously looking to the left, to the right, behind her—it was unbelievable, she couldn't get over it, these apparently tamed monsters, like contemplative angels for more than a second—never had the gift of such perfect attentiveness been offered to her.

"Just a second, Camiiyy, just a second....What's that diagram supposed to be, and the stars, all right, they're stars....But all this doesn't have anything to do with French, this is a French course, not a science course, remember?"

Camille, taken by surprise, looked at her. Before there had been speeches about Corey Hart, Wayne Gretzky, baseball, a weekend at Old Orchard. It seemed that the stars were the only ones unable to claim French citizenship.

"Keep going. Make it fast, but keep going."

"The Hertzprung-Russell diagram," Camille tried

starting again, "the Hertzprung-Russell diagram ...."

It was over. She had come down from her dizzying perch and turned back into a little girl with an acidulous voice, a skirt that wasn't preppy or mod or anything else, a timid mouse without mascara or bust, a girl they would have been ashamed to have given any importance to. Fat Marineau began to moo, "Spring-sprang-sprung," the Bouctouche brothers shot elastics at him, the menagerie let loose, sniggering and squealing everywhere, handsome Lucky Poitras started a poker game with his neighbour on the left. Mme Blotto said, "Sshhh," a few times, got up to scold the class routinely, but Camille had time to see, in the teacher's pale eyes, a glimmer of satisfaction. She folded up her charts and her colour illustrations and went slowly towards the door, followed by the now thundering voice of Mme Blotto ("Camiiyye! Come back here! CAMIIYYE?!..."), and didn't turn around until the heavy hand of the principal landed on her shoulder and roughly brought her back to this side of the Milky Way.

The rubber plant moped near the window. Its leaves had become bald, eaten away by a reddish rot, its stem had the air of having being conquered by a great, irreparable misfortune. Camille's eyes, fixed as an iguana's, contemplated the hairy chin of the principal. Nothing good could be expected from someone who let his plants die this way.

"Tell me if I'm wrong. This is the third time we've met, right? Is this the third time?"

His name was J. Boulet. He had been a psychologist in a previous career and he continued to use the smooth approach with his students, a modern method of causing disagreement without seeming to. He was a practitioner of active listening: for example, he would seize your last words and interpret them from every possible angle until something gave way, preferably in your head. The problem with Camille was that she didn't talk. Hard to actively listen to silence, even for an ex-psychologist.

"We met the second week of September, right? Do you remember that?...It was pouring buckets....What was that about, then?..."

He waited a moment, scratching his nostril with a mischievous smile. When he was convinced Camille wouldn't open her mouth, not yet, he started again.

"Oh yes. It was about a window, in chemistry class. A window you broke. But it was an accident, right? I think so."

"No," said Camille.

She was angry. Stupid bigmouth. Too late.

"No?" asked the principal, his eyes sorrowful, his brow puzzled, as though this were news to him. "No. It's true." He sighed. "Then the second time, what was it? Nothing important the second time, just some stupid thing? I can't even remember. That was two weeks ago, almost two weeks, right?"

He let a few seconds pass, stretched his feet out under his desk. Camille noticed that his two socks were not exactly the same colour.

"A question of disrespectfulness. With the math teacher. Correct me if I'm wrong. Would you like a candy?"

Yes, Camille thought, but she acted as though she hadn't heard. The bowl of cinnamon goldfish was passed quickly beneath her nose, then landed on the corner of the desk.

"As you like. I'll leave them there, in case you change your mind. They were my favourite when I was younger. What were we saying?"

He had just harpooned a couple of cinnamon goldfish; now he sucked them ostentatiously, no doubt to show her that he was still young, or that his tastes had stayed the same. Camille was suddenly afraid that he would keep her in his office for the whole afternoon.

"Three times," J. Boulet continued, his mouth full, his expression sympathetic. "Three times in a month and a half." Then, his torso aerodynamically tilted towards Camille, he attacked: "Maybe you're having problems. You'll have to talk about them, about your problems, if you want me to help you."

To oppose the force with inertia. To oppose the force with an inertia so profound that words bouncing off it are catapulted millions of light-years away from the school.

"I KNOW you have problems."

A leaf from the rubber plant fell to the floor with a limp sound.

"I only want to help you, Camille. Look around you, you're not the only one, there are plenty of others, children of single parents.... I mean, I know it's not easy not to have a father.... Do you want us to talk about it, Camille?"

He pronounced "Camille" delicately, keeping back his saliva and curling his lips as though about to taste a rare chocolate, his voice sweet and learned and nauseatingly sugared.

"I have a father," Camille cut in.

"You have a father? Okay. You're right. You have a father. I agree. I know a lot about you, Camille. Your mother does everything she can, believe me. Do you want to talk about it?"

To make sure he understood that the conversation no longer concerned her, Camille pivoted on her chair and looked out the window at a passing chunk of cirrus cloud that bore an amazing resemblance to a dog's head, or to billiard balls in motion, depending on the angle of observation.

"It's normal to be perturbed. You are perturbed. You are on a slippery slope, believe me....First the bad marks, then the lack of discipline, then the broken windows....That's the way delinquency starts. You don't want to become a delinquent, do you, Camille?"

Pause. Splinters of cinnamon goldfish disintegrated noisily between the principal's molars.

"Answer me. Do you want to become a delinquent?"

Camille looked at him. He had beautiful pale eyes wavering between grey and turquoise, a traitor's colour.

"I'd rather become a delinquent," she said, "than a school principal."

And now in the car. The persistent buzzing of a small fly imprisoned on the dashboard. The tense bumper-to-bumper traffic going nowhere. The honking for nothing, to increase the irritation; the blank faces of pedestrians. On the FM radio, voices that soar skillfully above the rush hour, commenting on a writers' colloquium or some other such exotic event. And Michèle's hands, which pretend to be patient, on the steering wheel, Michèle's hypocritical concentration, which is in fact entirely directed towards her, like a time bomb waiting to explode.

"This idea," Michèle began, "this idea of meeting right downtown."

Oblique looks, infinitely brief, directed towards Camille leaning against the door.

"Did you lock the door? I don't like you leaning against it that way, with your whole weight."

Rectification of the dorsal position and, while she was at it, partial lowering of the window to let the fly out, so at least one of them would be free.

"Are you sure you want to go there? Just because he was your father, you know, you have no obligation...."

"Yes, I want to."

Once again the offensive. Predictable.

"We're going to have to talk to each other, both of us, Camille. YOU will have to talk to me. Things aren't going well, not at all, at school. You always had good grades before, now you say nothing, you don't say what's bothering you, SPEAK TO ME!"

"There, I'm talking to you."

"Not like that. I want you to really talk to me. I want you to talk to me about yourself."

"Why? Everything I'm going to say, I know before I say it."

That stopped her. For a while they drove silently into the oppressive noise of the city, Camille's head nodding gently at the view from the car, as though to look beyond the buildings. Michèle's head was erect and stiff and filled to overflowing with dark speculations. She risked an insistent look at her daughter. Camille had not budged an inch, her eyes stared up at invisible objects and, above all, she wore an expression that frightened Michèle, a mixture of perplexity and absolute distress.

"What are you thinking about?" she asked, as gently as possible.

Camille would not answer, the evidence was there, inescapable: she had inherited all this from her father, the refusal to speak, the vagueness, the depressiveness, her pathetic marginalism. Then her daughter turned towards her and proved her wrong, one more time.

"One day," she said with a kind of smile, "there'll be nothing left here. The sun will go out just like any other star. Did you know that?"

FOUR

THE sun was rapidly setting on the terrace, above the heads that the chilly air was bringing closer to each other. Marie-Pierre felt a twinge of annoyance. She hated late afternoons, and the undeniable spectre of the winter that dared show its face a bit more openly with each passing day.

It would be necessary to wear more, an absurd platitude, to bind oneself in clothes which would no longer leave anything exposed to be seen. She liked to see people's golden skin disappearing into plunging necklines, she liked to look at bodies and their supple shapes—moreover she took great pride in her own, with its firm and triumphant breasts, so insistently protuberant no brassiere could contain them. At this moment, in fact, while she was greedily enjoying the tart flavour of her Campari and soda, she knew, without any boastfulness at all, that she was the most beautiful woman at the café, the most magically flowing and sensual. Beside her, the other women were tied up in knots, immobile, stiff and starched. The men were even worse, alas, icebergs worthily rigged out in their Lacostes and Guccis guaranteed not to fade in the wash. Marie-Pierre had a long-practised ability in microbiological observation. Humans, finally, seemed less sexy to her than viruses, and infinitely less skilled at making a place for themselves in the universe.

You just had to look around; people weren't living in their bodies, they were dragging them along like so many shameful diseases. They wrestled with their dermis and their epidermis, contrite and horribly confused to have a sexual organ, an asshole, emanations and secretions that spurted out without warning and ruined pretty clothing. The arm of the guy in front of her was afflicted with nervous indecision, kept switching from one knee to the other as though despairing of ever finding a spot to land; the girl across from him spasmodically started a loud shrill laugh that broke up in the middle; the shoulders of a young man, farther away, were so stiff they seemed to have been carved from stainless steel; the nails of another had been eaten to the elbow; legs, everywhere, apologized for existing and shrivelled up under the tables, eyes resolutely avoided straight lines; their words—a noisy elemental discharge—rushed madly about trying to camouflage the rest. Generalized abortions, gropings, babblings of invalids trapped in their skins. In spite of all this Marie-Pierre smiled indulgently at those around her, she was the sole being on this part of the planet who was alive and knew it—how sweet is human consciousness.

That was when John Turner appeared. He wasn't the authentic item, but a very successful duplicate, even improved, with something frank and saucy in his bearing. He sat down at the same table as Marie-Pierre. He smiled at her as at a young acquaintance from whom is expected, at the very least, the moon.

"You're very beautiful," he assured her.

Not a bad preamble, Marie-Pierre admitted to herself. Nevertheless, she didn't condescend to thank him, there are limits to feminine servility, but she did gratify him with a queenly look that served the same purpose. You're not so bad yourself, the part of her that never allowed herself to be passively picked up would have liked to reply, but she stayed silent and constrained herself to await the follow-up in a liturgical silence.

What would he come out with, how would he dress up the invitation to fornicate, with what frilly wrappings would he decorate the usual approaches—Can I offer you a drink What a beautiful day I've seen you somewhere before?

Oh, the tantalizing suspense.

"Last night," attacked Pseudo-John with a velvety voice and very beautiful lips, "I dreamed I was sitting on the terrace of a café very like this one. I was eating mussels."

Pig, Marie-Pierre thought. Mussel = lamellibranchia mollusc = very eminently vulvic symbol.

"They weren't exactly mussels, really, rather those small delicate whitish shellfish found in abundance on the east coast of the United States or the Magdalen Islands, you know what I mean?"

She knew. "Clams." Same sexual symbol.

"They were live clams. Talking, I mean. Every time I put one in my mouth it started swearing at me, in English, which was even worse—*you damned asshole, you sonnav-abitch, fucking bastard!*"

"Shit! I mean, 'By Jove!'"

"Yes, it was very irritating. I woke up."

He gave the waiter a subtle and aristocratic wave, ordered a Pernod with lots of water for himself, and nothing for Marie-Pierre.

"I'm not offering you a drink," he said, "because you'll think I'm trying to pick you up."

"Which is false."

"Which is true. But we have our pride."

"You are an Anglophobe, obviously, but you resist assimilation very half-heartedly, like all of us."

"Pardon me?"

"I'm talking about your dream. The clams that tell you to bugger off, excuse my French, do so in the language of Shakespeare, i.e. Westmount."

"Very interesting," he considered, inspecting his freshly arrived Pernod. "But just the same, I eat those English-women-clams, don't I?"

"Yes, but you are terribly embarrassed about it—at least, that's what you said," she excused herself.

"I didn't say 'terribly'," he smiled. "Do you know what I do for a living? You're going to laugh. I am the president of the Commission for Francophone Rights for the Individual."

She didn't laugh.

"Why are you looking at me like that? Don't you find me attractive?"

"Not really," she lied.

She was in a panic. Here it was, starting up all over again, her stupid heart jumping about, her bones going dangerously rubbery, and that sinuous heat at the top of her belly like a reptile... at forty years of age is it not ridiculous and unreasonable to let oneself be carried away by sudden infatuations? No, she decided.

"As for myself," John T. continued in his eiderdown voice, "I have to say that I find you extremely attractive, even very extremely, why not admit it?"

Yes, Johnny my sweet, why not, in fact, it's free and it's so easy to listen to. Marie-Pierre, unrivalled dissembler, showed nothing.

"What can I do to persuade you?" he inquired mournfully.

"Of what?"

"To come have dinner with me, for example."

"Impossible. I'm busy this evening."

That was the truth, straightforward and unchangeable, but Marie-Pierre was careful to emphasize the words 'this evening,' understand me if you can, follow me if you will.

"Then tomorrow?" he ventured.

"Maybe," said Marie-Pierre, with a Mona Lisa smile.

And then she got up. She wanted to go pee, that being the effect of emotion on her organism. She didn't simply walk to the washroom, she got there by gracefully rising, conscious, without seeming to be, of illuminating her passage with flames of concupiscence and admiring aggression. It would be a long passionate affair, something inside her was positive, no doubt he was married but she would accommodate herself to this superfluous and encumbering spouse who was hanging on to her ex-belonging like a fly to a turd—women can be veritable leeches when they set themselves to it.

When Marie-Pierre lowered her eyes, she couldn't believe what she was suddenly seeing: in front of her was a swollen object, hideously white, a porcelain monster that seemed to have been dragged out from her old nightmares. She stared at the urinal for thirty seconds of terror before realizing that this was no error, oh how human, without thinking she had gone into the men's room and all she had to do now was beat a retreat in order to wipe out *that*, that filthy thing from her past. She turned towards the door. Handsome John was at the entrance, looking quite stunned to find her here and with his fly already open. Marie-Pierre felt herself blushing to the filed tips of her nails, already blood-red, and wanted to flee after stammering a few unintelligible words including "wrong door" which came out sounding like meaningless babble. Fake John didn't step aside so she could pass. A hesitant smile had appeared on his lips and continued into the silence—petrified, you might say, by the comedy of it all. He advanced his hands towards her—to help her through the door, Marie-Pierre was actually thinking—and then stuck them right onto her breasts, which he began to knead as though working modelling clay or making pies, in brief, an effect with a maximum of surprise, and totally unpleasant.

"But, butbutbut," Marie-Pierre wanted to protest—but John-John didn't let go; his smile was now entirely lubricious and there was a moist sparkle in his eyes—"would you mind but what is this but STOP—"

"Your beautiful tits," he murmured in his silk and velvet voice, his hands digging in ferociously, "you've been wanting me to take them, eh, your beautiful tits...."

Marie-Pierre tried to push him back gently—look old boy, a bit of restraint, what the devil, maybe later, I'm not saying no—but he wouldn't stop pawing her, persuaded as he doubtless was that this was why she had been waiting for him in the bathroom, a slut who lurked beside the urinals so men would make passes at her, that was how he was thinking of her. In a rage, Marie-Pierre saw as red as the filed tips of her nails, and delivered him an uppercut that sent him flying onto the mediocrely cleaned, but very certainly hard, tile floor. Then she left, her hand aching but not as much as her heart.

She sat down again at her table, what else to do while waiting? She swallowed her Campari and soda in a single gulp, then the dirty bastard's Pernod, three-quarters full. She felt a little better, but not altogether; there are wounds to the morale that alcohol, unfortunately, is unable to cauterize. She hardly budged when he stumbled by her, the swollen remains of a grand passion that the waiters helped into a taxi.

It was cold. As she waited she became more and more depressed. Finally she saw a car stop in front of her and, bounding to meet her, an eleven-year-old beanpole, a very wide smile distorting her face.

"Hello, Daddy," Camille said, radiant.

"Shit," Marie-Pierre grumbled. "Why do you always have to call me Daddy?'"

FIVE

GABY was sitting in the control room, her face crumpling with the beginning of a cold and several sleepless nights, and she was dreamily observing the transsexual, a bit the way one lingers deferentially at the zoo, in front of a particularly repulsive apelike specimen.

In truth she was a strange creature, as peculiar as she was fascinating. Marie-Pierre Deslauriers—that was her name—had dressed for the occasion in a tight-fitting dress in indigo cotton that exposed her knobby knees and a sumptuously curved figure that would not have displeased Hugh Hefner in his younger days. It was, in fact, the mixture of bumps and undulations that plunged Gaby into mental disarray, and the show's producer, standing beside her, into hysterical giggles. Marie-Pierre Deslaurier's body seemed to be built upon paradox: in any case it lacked nothing, neither curves nor bones, the one continually bringing to the other a kind of surprising correction. Thus breasts and buttocks were rounded to perfection, but chaperoned by extremely athletic shoulders; a delicately featured face and soft hair framed a massive jaw; colossal hands, as wide as fireproof gloves, were manicured and polished and gracefully fluttering like frail twilight butterflies.

Most remarkable of all was what emanated, almost ferociously, from this hybrid creature: such a conviction of being fatally beautiful that it couldn't help causing a contagious stir all around. You looked at Marie-Pierre Deslauriers and were surprised to find yourself thinking that, yes, this...thing, woman or extraterrestrial, *was* beautiful.

The interview had been going for ten minutes, and Bob Mireau was already gulping down his second glass of water, in itself an event.

"If I'm following you correctly, Marie-Pierre," said Bob Mireau, "the body is nothing more than a deceptive illusion."

"That's not exactly what I said, my little Bob," replied Marie-Pierre with an enchantingly patient smile.

"Take me, for example. I seem to be a man, from the outside, at first, but perhaps deep down I'm a woman, in the deepest inner part of myself."

"That would surprise me. You seem to have all the basic characteristics of the macho male."

"Oh? That's reassuring."

"Aside from, obviously, various feminine urges that you are eager to hide."

"It's true," Bob admitted. "I always wear a bra to bed. But please don't tell anyone."

The producer, in the control room beside Gaby, emitted a long happy screech.

"What a total nut!" he moaned beatifically, without Gaby being able to guess to whom exactly he was referring. But she was starting to suffer from such a painful migraine that her natural curiosity was considerably dulled.

"For the benefit of our listeners," Bob continued, "tell me again some of what you've had to go through to become a woman."

"I *was* a woman," Marie-Pierre said again, very gently. "I simply had to rectify the physical anomaly that was my body."

"Indeed. The minor physical anomaly. All right. First, hormones. Lots of hormones, I suppose. You still take them, you'll have to take them for the rest of your life, won't you?"

"Yes."

"And then electrolysis—all that hair we men have, it would surely be a bit orangutan on a woman...unless you wanted to work in a circus or at the Ministry for Women's Liberation, I'm being silly, excuse me. Does it hurt a lot? First of all, were you very hairy? How many electrolysis sessions were necessary to give you that peachy look, Marie-Pierre?"

"Several," Marie-Pierre said evasively.

"Let's talk about the operation. That's essential, the operation: they take off the zizi and construct a female sexual organ, is that it? Incredible, there's no end to progress. Tell us a little about the operation."

"The operation worked perfectly. I am a woman in every detail. For example, I can have an orgasm in the normal way, in case you were wondering."

"Hmmm." Bob gave a brief chuckle, immediately imitated by the producer in the control room. "They say, it would seem you had to wear a kind...of...of mould, for a while, is that true? It's not that I absolutely have to get into the gory details, but you know, this kind of operation, for us normal men and women, I mean...biological...is a bit of a mystery. Is it also a mould, or silicone, that you have in your, in your chest?"

He finally stopped himself, to give the transsexual time to reply, after all, and because the twitching that was agitat-

ing the corners of his lips was very visibly threatening to
evolve into shouts of laughter. Marie-Pierre remained silent
for a few moments, as though absorbed by the noisy brilliance of her baby fingernail.

"If you like," she murmured, a wicked gleam in her eye,
"if you like, my little Bob, I could show you that in a bit, so
you could see what it's like with your own eyes.... Okay?"

"Impossible, my religion forbids it," Bob joked into his
glass of water, and Gaby saw him blush for the first time in
his life.

Meanwhile, in the control room, the producer and the
technician were exchanging metaphysical considerations.

"A hole, I'm telling you. That's all they can make for
them. My brother knows someone who had a friend who
had a friend who almost slept with a woman...a man, I
mean...."

"A hole! Lovely! That would be enough to make a guy go
limp...just a hole, cold and dry!"

Gaby, whose eyes were fixed on them, gave herself three
aspirins.

"So," she grumbled, "what difference would that make
to your sexual technique?"

"Tell us," Bob Mireau was saying in Studio B, "tell us a
bit about what this radical transformation has brought you,
Marie-Pierre...."

"I became myself. I am one hundred per cent me: you
can't say that much about very many people."

"That reminds me of something," said Bob, who was
endowed with a prodigious memory. "'All the resources of
science must serve the road to the self.' It was a Quebec
microbiologist, who was called Deslauriers just like you,
who wrote that—"

"I know," said Marie-Pierre.

"Did you ever meet him?"

Instead of a reply, Marie-Pierre smiled serenely. Bob Mireau turned terribly pale but, along with Gaby, was the only one to notice—that is why, among other reasons, he preferred radio to television.

"Since then I've given up microbiology," said Marie-Pierre.

"Just the same, you could have warned me," Bob said afterwards, annoyed with his poor performance. "A known scientist comes here, transformed into a woman, and no one tells me! How am I supposed to recognize her, operated on, sewn up, then stuffed with hormones like he's been?..."

Gaby claimed to be very sorry: she had known nothing about it, the creature had not mentioned a single word regarding this. It was Marie-Pierre who had telephoned to solicit an interview; at the time Gaby had been struck only by the sensational aspect of the thing and by the particularly rasping voice of the subject. Anyway, with this colony of crazies she had to turn away every day, how could she have time to pore over each of their *curricula vitae*? Bob, being a good fellow and having his mind apparently otherwise occupied, let the matter drop. As in every evening for the past week, he left the office with Priscilla, whose manifest charms must have more than made up for her inexperience. And Gaby was left all alone with her three telephones, her cat-piss-scented cubbyhole and the beginnings of a free-floating anxiety that now descended upon her at certain fixed times, as predictable as a bureaucrat.

Before leaving, the transsexual had come to shake her hand. The transsexual's hand was big and bony, made-up, and to the touch astonishingly smooth and embarrassing.

"We'll meet again," Marie-Pierre had smiled, very sure of herself. "We have interconnected atoms, you and I, an affinity of sister souls.... We know these things, between women...."

Then she had departed, leaving Gaby flabbergasted, her smile fixed, to marinate in an indefinable malaise.

Sister souls—feminine—she'd had them before. Friendships that were complex and volatile, then suddenly over because of the age that makes people treacherous or brittle, because of a quarrel, puerile as all quarrels are, because of a change of address. Because of nonchalance, because of the illusory feeling of plenty that makes it easy for us to drop familiar treasures, as though they were worthless glass beads.

Gaby, do you remember little Suzie Tremblay, her lunatic's face, her big surprised bird's eyes, her passion for blackballs and edible wax lips? You would make tunnels through the snow, wrapped in your waterproof snowsuits, hers always too big, moth-eaten at the knees and elbows, stretched out of shape by overuse and the systematic occupation of at least four of her sisters. You would invent passwords and feeble-minded games around these ineffable themes that were your favourites: poo, turds, bums. The joyous debility of the childhood you shared, the terrifying immensity of that minuscule yard that was your arena and your burrow and your inextricable Eden. The time she betrayed you with another, Gaby, and you wickedly prayed that the neighbourhood thief would punch her in the belly; and when she came back sobbing because she had just gotten, from the neighbourhood thief, a punch very precisely in the belly...(That's when you began to believe, do you remember, Gaby, in a God that was like a devil?...) And the time she cried while watching you leave without her, how to erase the remorse of that time that still occasionally niggles at your memory? You had promised her a drive in your mother's Morris, that ancient little wreck of a car that passed for a luxury in your neighbourhood, she had never set foot in a car, the terrible memory of her small girl's sadness and of your shame, Gaby, at suddenly understanding just how poor she was. Little Suzie Tremblay vanished into her life as a grown-up, taking with her the beautiful lunatic face of her five-year-old self....

Francine Duchesneau, Gaby. Prankster and giggler, so capable of following you into your extravagances and mystical epics: the haunted house you would visit at lunchtime, before going back to school, your hands laced together in the same audacious terror. Francine Duchesneau, who made you laugh so much that you wet your pants in the most unlikely places—those delirious pees that were a sign more of happiness than of an overfull bladder.... And when Francine Duchesneau's father died, do you remember her serious mourner's silhouette, seated docilely in the front pew of the church beside her family, the priest and his homily pathetic enough to wring blood tears from a statue, and suddenly she turned around, Francine Duchesneau, she spotted you in the midst of the first-year high school class, and you looked at each other for a long time, an interminable sad moment of hesitation, that whole disaster was so unlike her, you looked at each other and together, at the same time, the two of you broke into wild laughter. Francine Duchesneau, whose mother then scolded her so sharply, and who perhaps is still to be found wandering through other daydreams you don't know about, her beautiful laugh rebellious and free....

Michelle Lévesque. What vengeful present has got hold of her, Michelle Lévesque, who yearned for faraway adulteries, who sighed for the future, convinced it was her Eldorado? At fifteen she was a little chubby and already edible, and a sensation at every orchestral jamboree; sweaty handsome young men begged for the slow dances with her while you, you were left to pick up her crumbs, but you never held it against her because she always ended up leaving her suitors to come back to you...how can you not treasure the memory that in the end she preferred you to them? You would often sleep at each other's places, Michelle Lévesque and you, you would devour grilled cheese sandwiches at three in the morning and loneliness was forever abolished, you went cheerfully through the nights together, telling each other stories and blushingly whispering about those disturbing things that were beginning to stir in your bellies—it goes like THAT I tell you and the girl is underneath and depending on the angle it produces TERRIBLE electric shocks I swear it...so much more knowledgeable than you about these matters, she dreamed of going off with Prince Charmings who had tender voices but voluminous phalluses, Michelle Lévesque, and you, you only felt your heart contracting when you thought of that implacable future which would see her go away from you, oh, men already circling like vultures above your vulnerable friendships.

And her, your best friend at the beginning of the joyous seventies, Élaine Bossé, with whom you took more than one trip—acid trips or journeys to the end of the world—you were two atoms from the same molecule, mutual and fascinated witnesses of your first loves, your wild explosions, your hazardous navigations into the uncertainties and excitements of life. How high you flew together, and how softly you cushioned each other's falls, Élaine Bossé to whom you one day gave all your savings to help her get an abortion and who cried the tears of a wounded adult on your shoulder. Do you remember that magic moment, Gaby, when you two leaned against the rail of the boat that was leaving Ibiza, the light was bluish and mystifying, you squeezed hands and swore you would always stay this free and unattached? Oh Élaine Bossé, your more-than-sister, who now has three children and an accountant husband, and when you meet almost accidentally every two years around a few melancholy beers, embarrassed silences float between the insignificant nothings of your talk.

And there are still a few others, Gaby, names like white stones on your fierce Little Thumbelina road, Anne-Marie and Lucette and Myriam whom you see every now and then, buddies more than true friends, because the age of intensity passes like everything else and the time comes that you give only stingily of yourself for fear of not receiving enough in return. And women, now, as soon as they have emerged from their embryonic cocoon, hasten to weave another one from love, familial and totalitarian, and there is still more than one who disappears from the telephone directory, blotted out by the welcoming shadow of her spouse.

Thus did Gaby soliloquize in front of the sundry contents of a drawer emptied out on her bed. From time to time she would wrestle with these relics from her past, of which she had a large collection. Because, at the risk of blackening her character, here must be revealed a defect with which she had always been afflicted: she was a born kleptomaniac, or fetishist—Freud's disciples could not have decided between the two if they'd held a debate. Gaby had always had the habit of taking things from those who were closest to her, but as though against her will and without real dishonesty; it was often a question of trifles having no other value than belonging to someone dear to her. She only carried out this operation once for each person, which limited the damage; and the victims liable to attract her affections, and therefore her larceny, were few.

The drawer emptied out on her bed contained: a giant marble modelled on an apple core that had belonged to little Suzie Tremblay; a red plastic barrette that had held back the hair of Francine Duchesneau; Michelle Lévesque's first marine-blue kohl colouring pencil, which she had vainly spent a whole evening searching for—with Gaby's fraternal support; Élaine Bossé's bone ring; a black braided leather belt which was a relic of René; Bob Mireau's silver pencil; and a multitude of small articles surreptitiously subtracted from friends or occasional lovers judged worthy of this honour. Having reviewed these insignificant but disturbing fragments of her past, Gaby—otherwise so honest—felt a small stab of guilt. But far stronger and sharper was the pleasure of being in perfect contact with her memories, the pacifying certainty of being able to look backwards whenever she wanted, and to bring out the tangible remnants of her life.

Then Gaby put back her drawer and went to sit in front of Gudule. Gudule, although small, was endowed with a prominent green belly. Gaby had discovered her six days before, madly weaving a grandiose web in the corner of her window, and she hadn't had the heart to demolish such a beautiful work. For the moment, Gudule was occupied chewing the head of a juicy coleopter that Gaby had obligingly pushed into her web, but what would become of her when the cold wind blew and the insect era came to an end? Gaby was surprised to find herself worrying so much about Gudule, and this time she felt a very distinct humiliation: you had to have sunk horribly low to be hanging around with spiders this way...(suddenly the unbearable image of the Guatemalan prisoner tickling the chins of the scorpions in his cell to break the solitude). And since the night was young, she decided to call someone up—it didn't matter who, so long as she was female and fraternal.

It was Marjo. Marjo always turned out to be available, which made her simultaneously precious and despicable. She claimed to be a hard-line feminist, but as soon as a man's eyes turned her way she began to bat her eyelashes and waggle her posterior. That's how it goes, we're all lost in our contradictions.

They drank kirs at the Bistro and at the Café Cherrier, and ate duck steak at the Express. Marjo talked a lot, loudly, while Gaby bitterly eyed the very costly get-ups of the Montreal jet set. It seemed to her, as always, that her fall wardrobe was growing extremely unfashionable, not even worthy of the moths she had just discovered there. Finally, predictably, Marjo wanted to know every detail of the breakup with René, and out of duty Gaby told her the entire story, but she took no pleasure in it and anyway there wasn't much to say.

The evening was as flat as stale beer, as Élaine Bossé would have said in the good old days. But in spite of everything Gaby insisted on stretching it out, dragging Marjo to the Lux though she was numb with fatigue and alcohol, and burying herself to the point of nausea in masochistic meditations on the inanity of female friendships: what had she found in them up to now, oh Holy Virgin, that would justify getting stuck in sterile evenings that inevitably turned to gossiping and complaining about men, painful menstruation and the stupid irritations of their jobs?

"I could eat a horse," Marjo said suddenly, rubbing her stomach. Then she immediately added, as though upset at having violated some obscure principle: "a gelding, of course."

Gaby looked at her and gave a small perplexed whinnying laugh, doubtless because of the late hour, or tiredness, and Marjo also began to laugh, probably for the same reason, and suddenly they were irrationally carried away by a hysterical hurricane, a completely demented hilarity that left them twisting on their chairs, gasping and squealing, while beside them the waiter stoically awaited their orders. Marjo emitted ultrasonic squeaks, Gaby's sounds came more virilely from the throat, and this cacophonic duet repeated itself for five minutes by the clock, during which the disgusted waiter could have served ten other people.

Afterwards, when she had recovered herself, Gaby got up and deposited a big kiss on Marjo's forehead. Now she remembered why female friendships were so precious: it was only with women that you could have, so deep, so absolutely and marvellously free, that wild infantile laughter that can make life worth living.

SIX

WHILE Gaby, vanquished, finally gave herself up to sleep, Dominique Larue had entirely emerged from it because it was six o'clock in the morning. The light was still sticky, a dirty predawn glimmer, but it didn't matter; it was invariably at this precise moment that his imaginative day began.

Taking great care not to wake Mado, catatonically fastened to his left thigh, he got up. He proceeded to a few brief ablutions, then put on a pair of grey quilted cotton pants. In the huge dining room he peacefully attacked the 108 Taoist tai-chi movements that make a man like a cat and ensure that he communes with the cosmos. Instant perfection. His spinal column was wavering like seaweed, his belly hummed with energy and no sooner had he caught the tail of the bird and pushed the monkey to the bottom of the sea than his yin and his yang, those eternal antagonists, slapped each other on the back and lifted him, homunculus, to the dizzying spiritual summits beside which Annapurna is just a knoll and Everest a cross-country ski course for cowards.

Next, streaming with healthy sweat, exuding harmony by the noseful, he took an icy shower. His haemoglobin thus rattled, he sat down at his work table.

Part Two. And just six-thirty in the morning, please note.

He examined the white pages in front of him. He chewed the top of his new Bic. A moment of intense and painful reflection. What to write? What not to write? Suddenly it surged forth, a sort of groaning cumulus filled with tiny units of sound, a chaos of voices, it took hold of his hand, which started, all by itself, to darken the incredulous ex-white pages with words, sentences, complete chapters; and suddenly it all made sense, a magnificently complex fictional universe was springing forth in his head and he hardly had time to grasp it before the mental pages on which everything already seemed to have been written made way for other even more sensational and stylish pages and then for yet others, it didn't slow down, and he suddenly realized that all this time his skull had been pregnant with a titanic work without showing anything, even a suspicious bulge.

In brief, that's what they call inspiration.

And it was piling up, the room was strewn with papers splashed by his delicate feminine handwriting, it was a rising tide and his third Bic had just given up the ghost, quickly, a fourth so he wouldn't lose his rhythm—fortunately he had a supply of them, because foresight is always rewarded.

When it stopped it was eight o'clock and his right wrist was twice its normal size. Haggard, climbing over the stacks of his writing, he went to the window and stuck out his head to provide oxygen for whatever remained of his grey matter. Behold! there was his publisher, just passing by on the sidewalk and looking up towards him. Beside him was a pot-bellied man Dominique didn't know.

"Ah! My dear Larue," said the publisher. "Greetings, my dear publisher!" said Dominique. "How unexpected!" said the publisher. "How unexpected indeed!" Dominique returned. "My dear Larue, so, still nothing to show?" asked the publisher, as though intent on the rhyme. "On the contrary, my dear publisher," replied Dominique, announcing his crime, and he quickly gathered together the reams of paper covering the floor and offered them, in a jumble, to his publisher, like a bouquet of flowers tendered to a ladylove.

And the publisher read them, and the pot-bellied man was not ashamed to join in, reading over the publisher's shoulder, and then the right eye of the publisher began to glimmer with emotion and the left nostril of the pot-bellied man began to tremble with who knows what, and play it again, the fat stranger was in reality a producer of films with budgets as pot-bellied as himself, if you begin to grasp the incredible situation, from which only the cigar was lacking—this no doubt being the reason that Dominique's intuition, usually so acute, had been sidetracked—and at the same time both of them drew from their pockets voluminous contracts which, by another absolutely amazing coincidence, they just happened to be carrying. "I'll print fifty thousand copies of your book if you'll sign here right away," cried the publisher. "A hundred thousand dollars for the screen rights if you'll sign this on the spot!" the producer shouted. "Keep it down," Dominique laughed nervously, "you'll wake up my girlfriend."

And in fact that is what happened. Dominique was just getting ready to sign with both hands, while faking a vaguely disgusted nonchalance, when Mado, caressing his thigh, suddenly said, "What are you thinking about, lying there with your eyes open?" and Poof! fame and fortune slipped out of his grasp and he leapt up from the bed which, alas, he had been occupying the entire time.

•

It was thus this painful moment that truly began the day of Dominique Larue, who lived on illusions and a few earthly nourishments fortunately provided by Mado. Mado herself was getting up to go to work. First she gave him, on his thigh, the light caress that sometimes snaked higher, a subtle way of feeling out the terrain. This left Dominique embarrassed and Mado inevitably disappointed, because for a year Dominique had had various inert zones that did not seem to want to reactivate themselves. Then Madeleine got dressed, whistling as she did. What is the source of some human beings' infinite patience? How many times can a woman bear facing a sexual vacuum before assassinating her partner? That is the kind of unanswerable question that rose, frothy, to the mind of Dominique, and only slowly dissipated as he surveyed the beautiful, courageous, optimistic and now redheaded Mado rapidly going about the beginnings of her daily affairs. Take a lover, he would sometimes beg her, tormented by guilt. I love you, Mado would reply, with an unshakable smile. It was one of those comebacks that totally stunned him, because he didn't see how it followed. I lo-o-ve you too, he wanted to howl back at her, but in the present circumstances what good does it do, for that matter, what use is love against rattlesnakes, gale-force winds or bad breath, for example?

But Mado was convinced that for every ill there was an appropriate medication, and that Dominique's lack of sexual appetite would necessarily give in to the cure-all of love, with the help, of course, of a few psychotherapy sessions, for which she would magnanimously foot the bill.

In fact today was Thursday, T-day, for Treatment of the Soul.

Dominique never went. He had gone there once, four months ago. He remembered it well. The clinic was as sun-lit as a Club Med agency, completely devoid of all sinister connotations, though it was dedicated to the dark neuroses of the brain. The secretary-receptionist was good-looking and welcoming—but not too much so, which would have been suspect. The armchairs were of an agreeable Italian design, but not overdone, which would have been preten-tious. Everything had been planned not to frighten—jovial lithographs lighting up the walls, velvety piano music issu-ing from the loudspeakers, books of hilarious cartoons inno-cently scattered on the attractive tables, flowers, of course, masses of humble wildflowers looking as though they had just arrived from the peaceful countryside. Thus everything was intended to reassure, and that was what so frightened Dominique, this calm, this fake prettiness, where was this place hiding all the crazy people, why couldn't you hear pri-mal screams rising from the adjoining offices? Any kind of ugliness or noise would have been welcome to break this harmony, which he had decided to find detestable.

A plastic-coated woman in her fifties was the only other client. She was sitting in a corner as though in a trendy bistro, and he wouldn't have been surprised to see her eat-ing pastries while she elegantly sipped at her coffee—they did offer coffee, of course, which Dominique had rudely declined, without managing to tarnish the pleasant smile of the pleasant receptionist.

Then arrived the man whose supreme mission on earth was to help harden limp articles, or vice versa depending on the case—Dr. Frolette, his name a poem in itself—an acquaintance of the lover of a good friend of Mado and so Dominique's designated confessor.

The doctor gave the plastic-coated woman and Dominique a small nervous smile and started leafing anxiously through the files put on the corner of the desk by the beautiful and well-mannered child from the reception desk.

"Doc-tor Frolette," the beautiful and well-mannered child from the reception desk murmured softly, trying subtly to attract his attention, "DOC-TOR FROLETTE!..."

Dr. Frolette neither raised an eyebrow nor pointed the smallest eyelash in the direction of the unhappy woman, who once again murmured, this time in a voice sufficiently loud to melt down two hundred wax earplugs crammed into the auditory canal of an Australian sleeping several thousand miles away, "DOC-TOR FROLETTE!!!"

"Are you speaking to me?" asked the doctor, who had, in fact, beautiful eyes, lustrous chestnut hair and a sympathetic face.

Deaf as a post.

Dominique saw himself extended—or not—on a divan beside Dr. Frolette, in the midst of screaming out his most intimate erotic fantasies—"AND WHEN I WAS FOUR YEARS OLD MY MOTHER'S BREASTS, HER BREASTS!"—while from McGill Street to the Main curious strollers turned and giggled or, why not, gathered every week in front of the clinic to be sure they didn't miss any of the sequel, a sort of free weekly pornographic program.

No. Impossible. Dominique stood up.

"I forgot something. In my car." He smiled at the beautiful child and at the doctor, who smiled back, he must have only understood nonverbal communication.

He went out the clinic door, never to return. Dominique Larue, specialist in limp articles and classified escapes.

•

Mado didn't know. For four months she had believed, as firmly as some believe in the very mysterious mystery of the Immaculate Conception, that he was going to the clinic to receive his therapeutic due, and each week she held out fifty dollars to him for this purpose, and Dominique disappeared into the wallpaper for a couple of hours without saying a word, guilty silence.

He didn't go and drink up the money in a cheap west-end bar—which would have been boorish and anyway the bars weren't open yet, which eliminated that temptation. Because he had his principles he scrupulously retained almost all of Mado's money in reserve, so that one day he could offer her a gigantic gift—a mauve BMW with an ejecting front seat and a windshield that converted into a colour television—or just give it back to her, who knows, at the right moment. And he had chosen to consecrate the hour disloyally subtracted from Dr. Frolette to something very unpleasant, a method of self-punishment or self-sanc-tification or both at once.

He would visit his father. Every Thursday morning, from nine-thirty until ten-thirty. Sixty disastrous minutes, though passed in an undeniably stylish little apartment on Sherbrooke Street. Second floor to the right, door number 20, in front of which, no matter what the season, he had to wipe his feet carefully on the yellow straw mat to kill in the egg any bacteria that had dared stick to his soles, then leave his shoes, boots or sandals, even those cleaned right down to the threads, and in stocking feet or bare skin penetrate his father's three-and-a-half-room apartment, where his tor-ture truly began.

This Thursday, then. Dominique was getting ready to

ring the bell, having scraped his feet until they bled on a mat so vicious even a fakir would have complained, when the door opened wide. Maurice appeared in the doorway, more shrivelled than ever, his few hairs growing down over his neck, his eyes venomous—all of which was certainly part of his normal way of looking, but as though ornamented by a little supplementary something, a touch of curare or vampire-dog gall, it was hard to know.

"It's you," he said. "Ring the bell. Why don't you ring the bell?"

"I was about to. How are you, Papa?"

"You have to ring. How am I supposed to know it's you and not a bum or a killer? You know the city is full of them."

"All right, from now on I'll ring the bell more quickly. You seem to be in good form," Dominique tried, as a diversion.

"I don't like you scratching like that in the corridor, right in front of my door. Ring the bell. That's all I ask. Is it too much to ask?"

"No. Would you like me to ring it now?" Dominique asked facetiously, having great difficulty keeping his index fingers, his middle fingers, his little fingers, their upper and lower phalanxes, from committing the definitive deed—wringing the scrawny neck that bobbed just out of his reach, or just tearing to shreds what they were already holding, delicate chocolatines and almond croissants that had cost $2.50 each.

"HA! HA!" Maurice didn't laugh, but he moved back a few inches so his son could enter. "Are your feet clean?"

Clean. Clean like the vestibule, the yellow carpeting, the yellow underpad, the very ugly light fixtures, the armchairs with and without footpads, the undersides of the laminated tables, the rustproof taps and spouts, the insides of the toilets, in the decades and centuries to come, supposing there were still centuries to come in the wake of the daily pollutions and acids in the form of rain, no one cleaner than Maurice would ever be born on this planet. Dominique made coffee. Came and put it on the kitchen table where Maurice, sitting straight up in his chair, was with great defiance eviscerating a chocolatine, fork transformed into scalpel dismembering the pastry to isolate THE THING, this brown intestinal trickle that seemed to have ended up there because the pastry-maker wanted to show off, or perhaps he was just distracted. (A sudden image of little Maurice quietly playing with the defecations of his long-ago anal phase, starting exactly when and at what age, tell me the truth, doctor, do they regress down the muddy slope of childhood?)

"Chemical chocolate," Maurice decreed. "Synthetic, artificially sweetened, probably hormoned, yuck, that's it for me."

"There are some almond croissants," Dominique said without blinking, accustomed to worse than that.

"Almonds…HA! Have you seen anything resembling an almond inside that? Have you?"

"They're made with almond paste."

"It's all chemical. It's all been made so chemical that nothing is like anything anymore."

"It's true. How much sugar in your coffee today?"

"Four spoons. They're poisoning us a bit at a time. They're destroying our stomachs and digestive systems by making us eat these disgusting things."

Who are THEY? The Russians? The Quimperlois from Finistère? The Christian Brothers?

"These chemical products are going to kill us and no one says anything."

In two movements of his jaws and three quivers of his uvula Maurice swallowed an entire chocolatine, which, although synthetic, saccharined and hormoned, seemed to go down without causing too much damage.

"Life is chemical," Dominique offered, in order to say something filial and perhaps to finish the discussion, one can always hope. Maurice looked at him uncertainly, which in fact was the only way he had ever looked at Dominique.

"What are you insinuating?" he barked aggressively. "What does that have to do with anything? Why do you always have to say black when I say white?"

"Black?" Dominique said stupidly; he could not remember any discussion of chromatic nuances but the truth was, with his father the most benign conversation always turned dark and mournful.

He stood up, surreptitiously looked pleadingly at his watch—more than thirty minutes—and wiped all the crumbs off the table.

"Let's talk about you for a while," he said, prudent and magnanimous. "How have your heart liver insides been since last week? Have you seen the doctor about the pains whose exact location escapes me at the moment isn't that stupid but which were terribly painful I'm sure and what did he tell you?"

"Nothing," Maurice said.

And then he was silent. Usually he couldn't stop talking about this subject, he had this spear between his ribs, this worrying swelling on his little toe, this horrible buzzing in his eardrums, these spasms here, these shiverings there, the agony of Christ was a joyous ecstasy compared to his own situation, and Dominique complacently sympathized while thinking about other things and being thankful for the respite. And suddenly nothing. And still twenty-nine threatening minutes to kill.

"Should we go sit in the living room?" Dominique inquired—out of politeness, because in fact they were almost there, stretching out his right leg was enough to put him in the vestibule, and with his left arm he could reach the soap in the bathroom, it was a somewhat cramped three and a half rooms—but very clean.

"No," Maurice said unexpectedly, "you can leave, I feel a bit tired."

Dominique should have grabbed the ball on the rebound and whirled euphorically towards the door, he was being offered freedom, but he stayed where he was, his mouth hanging open, disturbed by something indefinable, something more weary than acrimonious in Maurice's tone.

"What's wrong? Aren't you feeling well?" he asked, gripped by genuine solicitude.

Suddenly, he was certain he felt it, Maurice's look was on the verge of crossing the barbed-wire fence he carried with him everywhere like a coat of mail; something was on the verge of happening between them. But didn't.

"I am feeling VERY well," Maurice spat out. "What I would like is to turn on the television, play a game of patience, be ALONE. Can you understand that? ALONE! Do you think I spend the week moping around waiting for you to bless me with your Thursday morning visit? EH?"

"No," Dominique coughed out.

He picked up his things and made for the door swearing to himself that he would never, by God, set foot in this place again, while knowing at the same time that he'd be back again the next week.

"See you next Thursday," said Maurice, who also knew it, and who closed the door almost gently.

In Mado's small Honda, which he had parked at an angle in front of a fire hydrant, Dominique turned on the radio and let himself break down crying, the way he did almost every Thursday morning. Into his memory came stale images from ridiculous movies where fathers and sons virilely clasped each other's shoulders, got drunk together or, idiots, cheered the exploits of some athlete whose sole skill was to know how to hit a puck that hadn't done anything to them. No matter. Dominique cried over this absence of everything, even of stereotypes, that was his relationship with his father. Then he calmed down. On the radio there was a voice that attracted him as soon as he heard it, a voice that had been his destiny for all eternity, he knew it with the first words it spoke.

"I became myself," said the woman's voice. "I am one hundred per cent me: you can't say that much about very many people."

Dominique, stupefied, noticed that he had gotten an erection. Like that, for nothing, his eyes still wet, his ears listening carefully. Absurd.

He started the car and began driving through the streets, searching for the woman whose voice, hoarse like after making love, low-pitched like a Brahms symphony about to take flight, had just—on his indifferent body—accomplished a miracle.

SEVEN

I T was nighttime. You could believe it was nighttime, even if it was only twenty-one and a half hours on the terrestrial clock, because the sky had been taken over by a black-and-diamond magic. Shining as though their light were coming through tiny perforations could be seen those capricious figures sketched out by the stars that man called constellations, in order to recognize them and give himself the illusion that he possessed them. Camille could easily make out Lyra, the Swan and Aquila, of which the brightest stars are called Vega, Deneb and Altair; farther to the east the pointed hat of Cepheus, the curved W of Cassiopeia and lower down, to the south, almost eaten up by the nevertheless minuscule Québécois metropolis, Pegasus, the immense geometric horse whose back foot is trampling Andromeda, who is hiding, amazingly, at the end of her only arm, a spiral galaxy much like our own.

GALAXY. An oppressive word that surpasses understanding. Our galaxy is the Milky Way, and although we are part of it we can, bizarrely, see it through its edge, those snowy filaments that swim above our heads. Almost all the stars visible to the naked eye—Deneb, Vega, Betelgeuse, Algol—belong, as does the sun, to the Milky Way. In space the Milky Way takes the shape of a huge spiral disk, a sort of gaseous saucer dragging us ever farther out, along with

150 billion stars and innumerable other floating objects. There are millions of galaxies like the Milky Way, spiral and brilliant, which turn in the inconceivable void and are constantly moving away from each other, each one made up of billions of stars and indistinct planets. A spectacle grandiose enough to drive the god who would observe it mad; we would like to be this god, even mad, for the infinitesimal space of a second, to grasp a little of the movement of the whole thing, to understand something, or nothing, of this vastness, and at least be able to see it just once and be forever consoled for our own finiteness.

While Camille was busy adjusting the eyepiece of her telescope, a shooting star went right under her nose. But she was not particularly moved by this—after all, shooting stars aren't real stars, just granite pebbles ridiculously small and close that burst into flames as they penetrate the earth's atmosphere. Far higher, above the visible, much more stupefying things are in motion: double stars, pulsars, supernovas, quasars, clandestine monsters that escape human logic and that Camille only dreamed of confronting. For the moment, nevertheless, she contented herself with tracking nebulae in the November constellations: NGC 7000, also known as America, was lurking somewhere, she knew it, between the flares of the supergiant star Deneb.

Whoever has not seen a nebula sparkle does not know what it is to truly marvel. As they ionize, nebulae, clouds of stellar dust and gas, take on supernaturally beautiful emerald and ruby colorations: there, in these elongated cocoon-like nurseries, compact and shining conglomerations of young stars are born. Nebulae are also involved in the deaths of small stars. When after existing for billions of years a small star dies, it gradually empties itself, exhaling, as though exhausted, its outer layers, which are held back by only a very feeble density; and then around its shining carbon heart appears a distinct halo, a round and evanescent cloud that slowly dissipates into space, but so slowly that in a thousand years those who are alive will still be able to watch it fading, a coloured arch in the sky, an open eye mutely crying out its agony; and those who are alive will say: look, a planetary nebula! If they still have the gifts of sight and speech, and of passion for things that are useless to them.

But the higher the eye goes, the steeper the descent seems when it returns to the flat place which is our own. Alas, Camille re-experienced this painful moment every time she pulled away from the telescope. Why were all the best things out there in space? Why? Why didn't someone keep a few back here, to cover over the usual disastrous everyday with something beautiful? The usual disastrous everyday was the suburban house a hundred yards away where Michèle was waiting for her, the VERY disastrous everyday was the compelling image of Lucky Poitras, which kept coming back to her and tearing her heart apart.

She loved the handsome Lucky Poitras. She loved him with a love that was wild, indissoluble and useless, she would have been better off with a wild love for one of Saturn's rings, or for Halley's comet, which only returned every seventy-six years. The handsome Lucky Poitras did not love her, he had sworn this to her and she had not died on the spot, such is the strange tenacity of existence. He had eyes as emerald as the oxygen clouds that undulate in the nebulous Triffid of Andromeda, and gold-coated pastilles for irises to which nothing else was comparable, even in the innermost depths of the intergalactic universe.

She had just been hiding the horrible sweater Michèle forced her to put on under her raincoat to protect her from the November weather in her locker—one characteristic of the disastrous everyday was that the most horrible things always turned out to be the warmest—when Lucky Poitras had come up to her. And had spoken to her.

Until now Camille had always looked at him surreptitiously. He wore clothes that were informal and expensive, he smoked American cigarettes and he played cards between classes. In spite of the fact that he was only fourteen, he wasn't caught up in adolescence like the others; he expressed himself with an ease beyond his age, people said his father was rich and it showed in his every gesture, that promiscuity with Mercedes cars and foreign countries. He also smoked hashish, and it was only on those occasions that he allowed the others to cluster around to beg a few puffs; the rest of the time he didn't hang around with anyone in particular, drifting among the older students, magnetically attractive, allowing a few girls in his wake but never for long, they could be found weeping behind their locker doors, cast aside like old banana peels. He excelled at poker—no one, even those in the fifth year of high school, was able to defeat him. He was a zero at school. A relaxed zero, which was not the least of his charms.

"I'd like to ask you something," he said to her without either preamble or smile, but had he added them Camille would doubtless have passed out.

"Me?" said Camille, so stupefied that her voice turned shrill.

"It's about those stars you seem to know so well."

He was leaning on the locker beside hers. Camille had his odour in her mouth, a mixture of leather, honeysuckle and blond tobacco, he exhaled a disturbing heat that went straight to her lower belly, a peculiar effect she didn't understand.

"They come into existence, stars, that's what you were saying?... That fat Bouctouche claims they just appear all of a sudden in the sky, overnight. But I say it happens like with any female: a star gets fatter and fatter, explodes—BANG!—and makes a whole bunch of little ones...."

He gave her a sideways smile; she was so stiff with tension she could only grimace back.

"We bet ten dollars on it," he added with a kind of amusement.

And he waited. Camille glimpsed fat Bouctouche on the other side of the row of lockers, he was pretending to be absorbed in the contemplation of his shoes but he was listening to every word of their conversation. Her self-assurance returned. Nowhere was it written that one of the miserable Bouctouche brothers would again witness her defeat.

"You are somewhat correct," she said, "but not completely."

She opened her locker door wide—the inside was covered with pictures—and then she set her passion free, finally, opening up as though she were by herself, without fear of ridicule, letting the words and concepts tumble out without reducing them, without simplifying them into babytalk the way she always felt she should (*The starsies are like treesies and beesies....*)

"You see, within the nebulae, which are clouds of gaseous particles, dust, residues of old stars, are Bok globules. Look: those black spots there, above the coloured zones. They're called Bok globules. And it is within those Bok globules that stars first appear, always clustered close together and extremely bright. It's thought that they feed off very dense particles found there, and that they are born through a gravitational collapse. In the Bok globules."

More than anything she loved to pronounce those sounds, *Bok-glo-bule*, she could have repeated them over and over, they were so like a password, a cabalistic formula opening the doors to the infinite. She contained herself. She had offered the key.

"But after that?" Lucky Poitras asked, looking her in the eyes. "Afterwards?"

"Afterwards? After that"—Camille caught fire—"each newly formed star frees itself from the gas in which it was born and goes off to live its own life, for thousands of years, burning off its hydrogen—that's what makes them shine—and then, bit by bit, when it has no more fuel, it expels its mass in the form of gas around its core—look how beautiful it is, it's called a planetary nebula—and that gas joins up with the gas of other dying stars and forms a new nebula, in which new Bok globules appear. Bok globules. The core of the star that has expelled its gas goes out peacefully, the star becomes a black dwarf. It is dead."

"Dead," repeated Lucky Poitras, his voice dark and lugubrious.

There was a silence, apparently meditative on his part and strongly emotional for Camille, because they had just shared this knowledge, however imperfect, about the destiny of stars, a knowledge beside which all other learning seemed derisory. Bouctouche had disappeared.

Lucky Poitras broke the silence. "I think," he said with a sudden laugh, "that neither me or Bouctouche gets the ten dollars."

He stopped laughing and looked at Camille with a confusing seriousness, she had to lean against her locker to avoid instant liquefaction.

"You're pretty smart for your age," he said to her gently. "Exactly how old are you?"

"Twelve and a half," Camille lied.

Lucky Poitras kept looking at her with a great sweetness, the unbearable brightness of the nebulae in his eyes.

"Pretty smart," he repeated gravely. "One thing for sure, I'd never want to go out with a girl as smart as you."

He'd left, after saying, "Thank you" and "Goodbye" very nicely, perhaps, she no longer remembered; she had stayed put, as though dead, with his honeysuckle fragrance and the throbbing question "Why? WHY?" in her throat. But she knew the answer, deep down—intelligence was a curse in this lowly world, intelligence was the reason she was left alone during lunch hour, in the evenings and summer vacations, to watch while others exchanged their happy nonsense; intelligence was a monstrosity when it occurred in girls and would condemn her to spend her life behind a giant telescope, alone like a wild woman. She had gotten the wrong sex and the wrong universe.

Clouds took over the sky before the America nebula had time to reveal its mystery, and Camille abandoned her telescope. She thought about her father. Her father with his pink smooth skin, his flowing dress, her father with breasts. It was he who had given her the telescope, a few months ago. Her she-father. More and more she, every time Camille met him. But always the same eyes in spite of the black liner on the lashes, the same attentive alertness; "My treasure," he would say, "my beautiful great treasure...."

Take me away, Papa, take me away.

Michèle's voice startled her from behind. "Good grief!

Camille! What are you doing? It's raining!"

Going back to Michèle's house. There was a hearth in Michèle's house, and a fire was roaring in the hearth.

"Would you like some hot chocolate? Would you like some popcorn?"

Michèle swung between excesses of solicitude and irritation. Camille preferred to remember only the latter.

"No, I have work to finish for tomorrow."

But out of pity she didn't leave right away. Lately her mother's hair had begun to turn white at the temples.

"I don't want," Michèle-the-irritated now insisted, "I don't want you going out before you've finished your homework, what time will it be when you get to bed? I don't—" Then, more gently, "What did you see in the sky?"

"Nothing. It was cloudy."

"I had an idea," Michèle said, rubbing her nose the way she did before proposing something serious. "At Christmas I'd like to take you skiing. In Switzerland."

"I'm spending Christmas with Daddy. He's going to phone you to settle the details."

Camille looked down. Michèle did the same. From the hearth the fire emitted an imbecilic crackling.

"He has no money, not a cent," Michèle muttered. "What kind of Christmas are you going to have? He has never given me a cent for you, NEVER!" she suddenly screamed with rage. "That madwoman. That EGOISTIC AND DEFORMED MADWOMAN!"

That was absolutely wrong. J. Boulet, who knew the human soul so well, had even advised her on this subject: even when justified, it was absolutely wrong to say bad things about the absent parent. Children always turn against the ones who say bad things.

"Listen," Michèle sighed, calm again. She took her daughter by the shoulders. "He doesn't have the right, legally, to see you. I authorize him to do so because of you, because I know you love him. He could harm you without knowing it, do you understand? It's dangerous for you to be around him, it's very dangerous for you, I'm not making this up, the courts have recognized it. He is a sick and disturbed person. Deeply disturbed."

Camille listened to her attentively, with a kind of respect. She is only eleven years old, Michèle suddenly thought, terrified, poor little thing already confronted with the monstrosity of adults, poor little tiny little child.

"You seem tired," said Camille. "You should go to bed. I'm going to work in my room."

Always the same nitwit exercises. Idiotic drivel that would eventually rot the brain. The direct object placed before after or during the past participle, the masculine always triumphing over the feminine—three thousand women and one pig went by—*trois milles femmes et un cochon sont passés*—acute accent and "s." Edifying algebra exercises, doubtless developed by a farmer from the last century with an imagination as fertile as his manure-covered field: How many kilometres and chickens are there in a train going between two rabbits? If a rabbit has three legs and a chicken eats one of them, how far from the train do the kilometres meet?

From beneath these insipid books Camille took out the text on quantum astrophysics she had borrowed from the library, and looked through it for a few moments, painfully concentrating: to tell the truth, this was not easy reading, constants and Planck's theory of absolute quantum units,

Drake's formula, positrons neutrons photons gluons, but slowly the light made a path within her, lighting up the cosmic enigmas concealed by the universe. Then she took up her schoolwork again, because that was where, unfortunately, she had to make her daily reckonings. She finished it off in twelve minutes and forty seconds, backed up by her quartz chronometer, and with disgusting pride considered the pages darkened by her awkward handwriting. It was all absolutely correct, that was certain, and it had all been so pitifully easy. Might she be a genius?

She laboriously recopied it all, this time taking care to put in as many errors as possible. In the kingdom of mediocrity, genius was something to avoid.

EIGHT

As you came in the corridor you could see nothing but corridor, and that was the way it stayed, because corridor was all there was in this bizarre dwelling—a long dark corridor bouncing straight to the toilet, scarcely deigning to widen along the way to permit the restrained display of cooking and sleeping paraphernalia. Marie-Pierre felt as though she were inhabiting a trench, or the digestive tube of some rectilinear monster. This was not necessarily disagreeable; you could look over your possessions in a single glance and, if you were in the mood, you could devote yourself to bowling, boules or, why not, bicycling—in brief—the tunnel was a veritable château. Moreover, she didn't live there alone; a colony of silverfish also appreciated the place and didn't hide it, one hundred and sixty-nine, she had counted them one insomniac night because it was especially at night that they could be found going about their business, doubtless in order not to disturb the principal tenant, considerate little beasts at heart, but immovable just the same, she might perhaps have cherished them like sisters if they had paid their share of the rent, but they didn't.

Marie-Pierre crushed three of these animalcules, lost or sleepwalking, while putting her bag of groceries on the table. Inside the bag were rice, potatoes, coffee and pork sausages—the wherewithal to survive the next two weeks.

She had stolen the pork sausages at the last moment, suddenly remembering that she liked meat and that there was only six dollars and seventy-five cents left in her purse. Now she told herself she would have been better off taking calf sweetbreads or filet mignon, once she was risking degeneracy. But that was the way it went, petty scruples had intimidated her, or maybe it was cowardice, because the premium items must be more carefully watched, an infrared alarm concealed in the haemoglobin of the filet mignon, a flashing light set off by a dishonest hand on the vein of the sweetbread, you never knew to what depths technology could drag these stingy supermarkets.

The day had been perfect, i.e. consistent with everything she had been going through for months: no heart palpitations to worry about because of shock or surprise, they were always a given. She had gone to the Ministry of Social Affairs. There, a phlegmatic suit pretended to listen to her for an hour, then abandoned her to another suit—not very nice, that one, he hadn't pretended anything at all, not even to be interested in her case.

For almost four years now, Marie-Pierre had been coming up against the hostility of this vast uniformed brotherhood that she had never before noticed, the omnipresent dark power. The suits. The suits were everywhere: in universities, laboratories, companies that refused to hire her, ministries in which her file was manipulated with arrogant disdain, media that mocked her existence, no doubt she would never be absolved for having dared to leave their ranks to join the rearguard of weakling and subordinate females.

For almost four years now, Marie-Pierre had been trying to have changed, in her file, the letter M, which classed her with the male sex and which, perpetuating itself on all her official documents, caused her innumerable difficulties. One letter to change: the time of a keystroke, the batting of the eyelid of the secretary in charge of the word processor, nothing at all, or so little.

Not so easy.

One of the first government suits to whom Marie-Pierre had made her request four years before had maliciously challenged her: "Prove to me that you're a woman!", to which Marie-Pierre had maliciously replied, "You prove to me that you're a man!"

There ensued a long administrative doze.

Armed with the written declarations and expert testimonies of surgeons, psychoanalysts and other medical specialists who had examined, studied and operated upon her, and who attested to her total Femininitude, she had presented herself numerous times at the Ministry, had met with numerous suits because her case appeared ticklish, in fact aggravatingly so, and apparently required numerous expertises. A suit more inventive than the others had finally objected that, since the operation had taken place in the United States and the doctor was American, his claims could not be considered credible; moreover the American dollar was only going down relative to the yen and the mark and a space shuttle had exploded in mid-flight and Canadian-American free trade was crushing everything like an elephant's foot, in sum, there you are, why hadn't she gotten herself mutilated, excuse me, operated on in Canada land of our forefathers, which would have been different and more patriotic?

Marie-Pierre had immediately returned to the fray, this time armed with the written declarations and expert testimonies of Canadian specialists who had bent over the *corpus delicti* and attested that, yes, alas, this ex-man was now, medically speaking, a woman, and that this must be recognized.

There ensued a very long administrative doze.

When she telephoned the Ministry, those in charge of her case were never available and didn't take the trouble to return her calls, and when she went there in person, a terrified undersecretary delegated by her superiors told her that her case, if you please, was under review and that she only had to wait quietly if you don't mind preferably outside if it's not too much to ask.

Marie-Pierre, having finally detected a kind of dead end, had then sent the following letter to the Supreme Suit of Social Affairs.

Honourable Minister,

I am daring to address myself to you because you appear to me open, resourceful and capable of resolving the delicate dilemma in which I find myself. Here it is. I am a Monster. This has nothing to do with my outer appearance, which I ask you to believe is especially seductive; it has to do, instead, if I have correctly understood the statements of your distinguished officials, with a very rare form of monstrosity, entirely internal and cerebral, which unfortunately makes it incurable.

A few years ago, for serious reasons I wrongly thought concerned me alone, I decided to change my sexual identity. After long and painful treatments, which it would be too distressing to enumerate here, and a series of successful but horribly burdensome operations, I became A Woman. That which I then believed to be the end of my existential problems turned out to be only the beginning, so it is that optimism is one of the great human weaknesses, like pride and the insane desire to eat excrement.

Your distinguished officials, whom I have not the presumptuousness to think ill-intentioned, are amicably driving me into extreme poverty.

On the one hand, by refusing to change the clause in my official papers that attests that I am of the M sex, they guarantee me perpetual unemployment: it must be understood that no employer, even one with normal preconceptions, would agree to hire someone he sees is a woman but reads is a man.

On the other hand, the distinguished official in charge of Unemployment Insurance, which I know is not within your jurisdiction but whom I quote for your amusement, refuses to grant me benefits on the grounds that transsexuality, which he must be confusing with malaria, is a disease and that disease is not admissible, etc. Moreover, the distinguished official in charge of Social Welfare, who is indeed within your jurisdiction, also refuses me benefits because in his opinion I am able-bodied, thus capable of holding a job and not admissible, etc. This makes a lot of objections, for just one person, and very little money, if you will forgive me this indelicate pragmatism.

I have finally understood the reason your distinguished officials have refused to strike from my file this untoward M which is keeping me from my daily bread, and I sympathize with their embarrassment. It is that this untoward M does not refer to my ex-status of MALE, as I in all innocence believed, but to my new status as MONSTER, a specification that I realize they wish to conserve because things and beings must be called by their proper names.

I certainly will not hide it from you, the life of a Monster is hardly livable, and I am therefore inclined to disappear elegantly in order to facilitate the digestion and repose of all your *distinguished officials. This is the point at which I have arrived in the delicate dilemma I mentioned to you at the beginning. An annoying congenital honesty makes me reluctant to commit illegal acts; and suicide is an illegal act, if I am not incorrect. How can I arrange to disappear in a legal fashion? Are there government services I don't know of that specialize in this? Might they be prepared to proceed with elimination for a reasonable fee, which I could try to get together by selling my two gold molars?*

I await your judicious advice with respectful impatience, as the time has come for me to bring this problem to an honest resolution.

> *Yours sincerely,*
> *Marie-Pierre Deslauriers*
> *Doctor of Genetic Microbiology*
> *Winner of the "Brain of America" Prize, 1977*
> *Candidate for the Nobel Prize, 1979*
> *Ex-Professor of Applied Microbiology*
> *Ex-Director of the Canadian Centre for Contemporary Research*
> *Ex-Human Being*

The minister had replied without delay, because at least he was a decent man, he just needed to be reminded of it from time to time, like all those rendered forgetful of their natural virtues by the exercise of power. With praiseworthy stubbornness he tried to reach Marie-Pierre several times, but Marie-Pierre no longer had the use of a telephone at her apartment, or of all those public utilities that make humans comfortable and unlike beasts. A letter from the Minister finally reached her; he excused himself personally at least four times for the actions of his employees, he offered reparations, he sent her an official certificate attesting that she was a Woman and should be considered as such, with copies sent to all the relevant services within his jurisdiction. That was well and good and delectable to read, but at this juncture an election came and the supreme suits of the existing government scattered like corks from cheap champagne, to be replaced by new suits opposed in principle to all the directives of their predecessors, and everything had to be begun again.

The last minor assistant-director she had met today had just been made part of the Brotherhood, and he had no intention of wasting his time on pointless amenities. Yes, he had carefully gone over Marie-Pierre's claims, and he understood nothing: why wasn't she grateful for a society free enough to tolerate her existence while other countries, not so far away I assure you, would have parked the authors of similar crazy fantasies in unnameable ghettos? Of course she had no money, but whose fault was that, after all those fiddlings with chromosomes and sawings off of phalluses by those overly expensive charlatans, you might at least, goodness gracious, we have to accept the consequences when we do something so unthinkable, but all right, we aren't heartless, we'll see what we can do my little lady.

My little lady. He had added that spontaneously, while giving her a pleasantly condescending smile, because after all she had nice eyes and a figure that could fool anyone, so this was the exact tone, half-reproving, half-caressing, that suited little ladies, and Marie-Pierre saw herself behind a desk like the one of this suit, the colossal respect she used to read in all the doggy eyes raised towards her and yet she was the same person, the obsequious courtesy with which people would speak to her and yet she was the same person,

would the Director be so kind as to glance at, might the
Director be willing to meet the delegate from the European
Community, the President of the United States would like
to know the Director's position regarding....and those triumphant salvos that greeted the least of his discoveries, the
most infinitesimal of his writings, and in the evening he
would be served truffles from Périgord, Gevrey-Chambertin
and tender venison steak with marrow and Madeira sauce,
only ten years ago but like a previous life, and yet inside she
had stayed exactly the same, and now there was this dismal
hole in the south end of the city, rice at every meal and this
unbearable haughtiness in the voice of those zeros who
didn't even come halfway up her ankle.

My little lady.

Marie-Pierre concocted herself a dish of rice with sausages
and soy sauce. She ate it slowly, twisting her face into
expressions of gastronomical delight while thinking of the
Third World and the infertile deserts in which people have
to eat grilled grasshoppers to survive. When threatened by
despair, it was enough to think of the Third World. And the
mirror.

At the extreme south of this long and narrow apartment
that a recent waitressing job had permitted her to keep until
now, Marie-Pierre had hung a mirror. Right on the bathroom door. It was a mirror with a wooden frame, very simple and very tall, where she could see herself any time she
deigned to look in that direction.

The mirror tirelessly repeated to her that this body was
hers, that after years of painful indecision, duped as she had
been by malevolent gods who had wrapped her in shrouds
she had never stopped struggling against, even and espe-

cially during the days of honours and ridiculous glory, this
fabulous body had finally been given to her. This was her
real and tangible glory—daring to look like who she really
was, despite all the righteous-minded who were so sure of
themselves.

After eating, Marie-Pierre placed herself in front of the
mirror so it could repeat its soothing message, because the
night was coming down like rain, and in the dark the body
can do nothing for a mind that is vulnerable.

Suddenly, on the shimmering surface of the mirror, she
saw him appear behind her right shoulder and detach himself, white and grey. Like her he was standing opposite the
mirror and was contemplating himself, but with a touching
bitterness.

All she had to do was close her eyes; then he would have
to go away, ghosts have no hold on real life.

She closed her eyes. Opened them again. He hadn't
budged. On the contrary. He had put himself between her
and the mirror in such a way as to exactly intercept her
reflection, and he was looking at her. Pale irises, illuminated by a fearful aggressivity. Now she must resist her inner
tremblings, stay strong despite the horror, because this kind
of confrontation could irreversibly destroy her equilibrium.
She had known he would appear sooner or later, more than
once she had sensed him lurking.

"Get out of here," she whispered.

He laughed. Not quite a laugh, a kind of rusty cackle
that frightened her even more. His harsh laugh, that she
thought she had forgotten.

She pretended not to know he was there. Deliberately
she fixed her hair in front of the mirror, as if, having become
transparent, he could no longer get in her way. Her eyes

were in his eyes, a terrifying face-to-face she absolutely must win.

"Slut," he said. "Goddamned slut."

Smugly, with a shaking finger, she went over her eye makeup, lightening her brows, working on the tips of her lashes, meticulously scratching at some dry skin encrusted on the side of her nose. He did the same, imitating and anticipating each of her gestures, transforming them as he went along into a lascivious caricature and burlesque, his haunches swaying from side to side, cooing and murmuring, until she couldn't take any more and turned, terrified, from the mirror. But he was also behind her, with his harsh giggle and his desperate eyes. She fled to the bathroom, where he arrived before her, urinating noisily into the toilet, shaking his little penis with disgusting enthusiasm.

There was no getting out of it, she had to confront him.

"What is it you want? What do you want, for the love of Christ?"

"Look at you," he mocked, advancing towards her, "look what you've done, how ridiculous you are."

He was wearing an old white smock, grey flannel pants—his laboratory clothes, worn and yellowed with acid stains. She stood up straight, in her high heels she was taller than him.

"GO AWAY!"

"Everyone makes fun of you," he sneered, his hands in the pockets of his dirty smock. "Look what you've turned into, a ridiculous old slut...."

"But I, I am ALIVE, and you, you are DEAD, dead...."

He was close to her, very close, she could see the way his cheeks were being eaten up by his encroaching beard, the prominent bones around his eyes, there was the familiar smell of carbolic acid, and his pale eyes, she didn't want to look at his eyes, his eyes so pale and so bitter, she must not linger on the eyes.

"What did you do to me?" he suddenly asked, his voice knotted with emotion. "Why did you do that to me? Why?"

He began to sob, his hands twisted into his smock, and she saw his Adam's apple jump and wrinkles of sorrow digging into the corner of his mouth.

"Why did you kill me?" he sobbed. "Why? Why?..."

Marie-Pierre took her leather suitcase, the only thing she had left from her previous life, and hastily stuffed it with all the clothes she possessed.

She went through the door of the apartment-tunnel, closed it behind her and ran. But even when she was far down the street, she could still hear the sobs of Pierre-Henri Deslauriers, that desperately unhappy man she had been.

NINE

H E was wearing the red leather jacket, the one with the so-called "bat-cuffs," designed in Milan, for which she had unhesitatingly paid $595 plus tax and which she had given him in that inconceivable time when they lived together. Inconceivable and recent. He was also wearing calf-high boots of black doeskin for which she had bargained like a madwoman in a Paris boutique and for which she had finally been ripped off to the amount of $300 American, which she had hastened to give him on her return from the trip, in that same inconceivable and wasteful era. And look, one of those pairs of unbleached cotton pants she gave him every two months because he had an intense passion for beautiful clothes, poor thing, and couldn't get them for himself.

Gaby wondered, not without cynicism, if under the unbleached cotton pants he was wearing a pair of those fetching and expensive briefs she used to supply, that make the male groin appear so desirable, and, while she was at it, if in his jacket pocket he was carrying the last safes from the king-size box she'd also paid for.

The girl beside René—doubtless still unaware of the high quality of his briefs and super-lubricated condoms— was visibly appreciative of the red jacket, the doeskin boots, the unbleached pants and maybe also, why not, the being to be found at the very heart of all these beautiful things. Gaby too had once loved the solidity and tension of that body, and the slightly arrogant regularity of the face; but in the end, of course, she could see only the arrogance of both the body and the mind.

René. He was putting himself out to charm this girl, the one beside him, an easy enterprise since the outcome was no longer in doubt. Through the good graces of a sympathetic friend, Gaby knew that René had moved in with someone almost immediately after their separation—a wild and passionate affair, said the sympathetic friend—and now he was living out love's sweet dream with a woman older than himself (and richer, Gaby had silently added, to amuse herself). And he was also making up to women in bars, just as before. As always, the older woman would be at home biting her nails, unless, being perfectly liberated, she was having it on with various convenient lovers.

But all that should have left her cold, amused, an untouched iceberg; their own relationship had long grown stale, had taken place in other decadent centuries, and furthermore it was she, triumphant conqueror of fate, who had struck the final blow. But it wasn't dead at all: the iceberg was grinding her teeth, the triumphant conqueror was having homicidal thoughts. That outmoded creature down there, holding forth at the other end of the bar, whom she'd gotten rid of like a torn pair of panties, could still fill her with hate. She watched him as he moved his lips, lit a cigarette—look! he had started smoking again—comfortably leaned his elbows on the chrome counter, aware of his good looks and the fact that he was getting away with trying to pick up that poor idiot woman; in short he was alive, and the old rancour sprang up in her. The bastard, his confidence had come back quickly enough. Only those of great spirit, it has to be said, are capable of great sorrows (how she loved this maxim, which sprang into her brain from whom or where she didn't know, perhaps she had just made it up).

Suddenly he saw her. She neither smiled nor turned away her eyes, they exchanged something brief, invisible vibrations at ground level. He was the one to turn away. At that providential moment, Bob Mireau emerged from the washroom. He had hardly perched himself on the stool beside Gaby when she pulled him towards her, her fingers on his neck and her hips seductive. If he was surprised he didn't show it, and he kissed her with appropriate passion. Bob was a pragmatist who knew how to seize opportunities without asking useless questions. And it worked. Finally! Gaby saw the vacillation in René's smile, she knew he was watching them and couldn't stand it—all that without having to really look at him because, after all, their former intimacy and ex-mingling of minds must be good for something. Five minutes later he left the bar, a flash of red leather zigzagging towards the exit, the girl perhaps on his heels but it didn't matter, Gaby felt a brief transitory joy which lasted long enough to soften part of the evening.

Bob, however, unconscious of everything else, ordered his fifteenth gin and tonic of the day and another lemon Perrier for Gaby. All the alcohol he had been ingesting for years must have finally made a pact with the other liquids in his body, because nothing ever showed, he had the smooth colouring of a Tibetan monk and a paunch only slightly rounder than average. They had left the studio together and found themselves in a Rue Saint-Denis bar, passing the happy hour with an alcoholic aperitif, then passing several more hours in pure alcoholism. Gaby, endowed with a fragile liver, had needed to top off her drinking with something less offensive. It was almost midnight, neither of them had eaten and now it was too late to worry about that, they had drunk so much they were overflowing.

The conversation picked up where they'd left off, despite Gaby's growing stupidity and the curious little wrinkles that had suddenly appeared on Bob Mireau's smooth forehead.

"What were you telling me," he asked, "about that mad-woman, that transex-transit, that hormoned-up thing?"

"Marie-Pierre Deslauriers?"

"Keep going."

"The telephones haven't stopped ringing. People are shocked, scandalized, they've been calling for two weeks to complain, to ask 'who is that, how can such things happen, they can't happen, can you—,' etcetera. In brief, victory. Henri wants us to have her back."

Henri was the producer.

"Ah well," said Bob, surprisingly indifferent.

Things weren't going so well, apparently, despite the fif-teen gin and tonics and the incredibly dynamic looks he affected towards the creatures orbiting in their vicinity. Gaby wondered if she ought to pose a friendly question, or pretend that she didn't notice anything unusual. She opted for pretence, which doesn't demand anything and doesn't advance anything, but is so restful. The conversation began to wilt. Moreover, they weren't obliged to talk, why insist when the blaring music takes care of everything? Bob got up for the nth time and pointed himself towards the wash-rooms. Maybe he was sick, Gaby worried, but she remem-bered that there was a telephone booth beside the wash-rooms and resigned herself to another night of going home alone. Worse catastrophes than that had been let loose on the world, after all, and solitude would provide her with the opportunity to continue the vast and complex comparative study of different kinds of chips she had launched a few weeks before. She had already arrived at a few preliminary conclusions: that wavy Hostess barbecue chips are less crunchy than Pringles cheese, that O'Ryan's sour cream are tastier than old-fashioned Humpty Dumpty and that all of them, alas, leave back-stabbing crumbs in the bed.

When Bob came back from the washroom—or the phone booth—his face was so darkly upset that this time Gaby felt she had to say something.

"Anything wrong?"

"What do you mean?" he said, stricken.

"I don't know, you're, you, well, you're not feeling that great, are you? But there's no reason you should talk to me about it, obviously."

Obviously. A couple of ice cubes that had strayed between Bob's jaws began to make an appalling cracking sound.

"Are you still seeing Priscilla?" she tried, at random.

"Who?" said Bob, and Gaby knew she had touched a nerve.

She let a few seconds pass, diplomat that she was. The bar was floating in a comforting cacophony—*gimme a break, gimme a bloody break*—the loudspeakers roared, and the crowd came back with enthusiastic onomatopoeia while the lapidary phrases, heavy with consequence, bounced higher and higher, a whiskysodatwokirsthreeBradorspillsPILLS!— all together in a postmodern symphony to delight perverse music lovers, who are legion.

"A pretentious stupid little bitch. Thousands of others

like her. Stupid, pretentious and interchangeable."

He had spoken as though talking about something else, with an oblique smile in the direction of a slender young woman who had just brushed past him and returned his smile—"I saw Bob Mireau at the Paquebot yesterday evening," the young woman would tell her friends tomorrow, or "I slept with Bob Mireau last night," perhaps, but no he wasn't interested in that, because he turned back towards Gaby as though to pursue a vital exchange or seek her approval.

"Were you talking about Priscilla?"

"Among others." Bob smiled, and in this smile there was a great distress he no longer even tried to conceal.

Gaby took his hand. It was all she knew to do on this sort of occasion.

"It's not true," Bob Mireau sighed. "It's absolutely not true."

"What?"

"That she's stupid. She's wonderful, Gaby, she's really a VERY wonderful woman who doesn't want anything to do with me, nothing at all."

He had ordered another drink, had already half emptied it, and his hand was trembling slightly as he set it on the counter.

"You must be kidding," Gaby said. "You were always together."

"Yes. You said it. We were. And now—we're not. She finds me stupid and pretentious. And she's right. I am stupid and pretentious. And interchangeable."

To that last statement he drank, with a triumphant laugh. Gaby, upset, ordered herself a triple cognac. What can an insect do for a mammoth's sorrow? That was how she had always seen Bob Mireau, a monster of serenity and good fortune, while she seemed born to an endless struggle with life.

"She reads *Marie-Claire* and *Reader's Digest*," Bob Mireau continued. "She's a federalist. She's a terrible cook, cheese-topped hamburger in margarine, boiled cod stuffed with tofu and bananas. Can you see me, me, eating boiled cod stuffed with tofu and bananas?"

Not easily. Although.

"But she's got me. She's got ahold on my insides. I've never felt like this. I do terrible things I've never done before, I send her dirty presents and love-struck letters, I telephone her at night—look, I've called her ten times tonight and she hasn't answered, the bitch, I know she's home, I can't do without her, Gaby, can you understand that? She sleeps with other men and I imagine myself assassinating them, I'm losing it, if you want to know, I'm going nuts."

Serves you right, Gaby thought for a moment, despite her very real compassion.

"But what happened?"

"Nothing. Everything was great, smooth as butter"—margarine, Gaby corrected silently, with a touch of malice—"and suddenly she withdrew. She says she's still young, she wants to step back a bit."

"So it's temporary, nothing that can't be cured...."

"So you say," Bob laughed sadly. "Do you think I haven't heard that before, that stupid line? I've used it often enough myself to get rid of women I didn't want."

Gaby looked at him, amazed that he wasn't more struck by the unexpected humour of the situation. But no, Bob Mireau, ex-sparkling radio host, seemed to have become insensitive to the comic twists of life.

"Things will work out," she said, without really believing it.

"You think so?" Bob said. His face lit up with adolescent hope.

He got up, almost calm again. Suddenly sixteen and a half years old, with an irrepressible desire to once again try the impossible: he was going to go to Priscilla's place right now, this situation couldn't go on. He paid for their drinks and, before leaving Gaby, had a burst of virility.

"Of course this is between us, okay?"

"You know me. A tomb."

"You're a pal." He kissed her on the neck.

Gaby smiled sardonically. "Thanks."

Now there remained only one choice to make: either to stagger back home and gulp down the two bags of barbecue Doritos she hadn't yet tried, or to pick someone up.

Pick someone up, then. But how? Since she had been peacefully coupled, the techniques and the locations had changed without her really noticing. Before, when she was young and crazy, she had excelled at the game, but back then the bars were quiet, people sat almost opposite each other or leaned very visibly on the counter, the sweet murmur of the music made it possible to start up epic conversations with interested parties that ultimately led to bed, yes, but by so many cerebral detours that you emerged reassured of your own intelligence—and thus disposed to let the body loose. The Neanderthal Era.

Now you had to make your way by force, dealing out a few punches when necessary, just to get to the bar and all its surrounding racket, and stand there, an idiot, not seeing anything or anyone because of the demented crush of human bodies—unless you had screwed your rear end onto a stool early in the afternoon and hadn't budged since, which Gaby had done opportunely. But even sitting down and anchored by various kinds of alcohol, how could you recognize a soul-mate, or at least a sex-mate, in these multitudes? And how, once recognized, could you attract its attention?...

For example. For example that guy over there alone, beside another who was alone, both of them surrounded by couples and both glimpsed by way of the big blessed mirror. The first one attracts madame, he has the cheap look suitable for the moment, let's say. All right. What does madame do to signal to the reflection of the cheap looker: Come over here, I don't hate you.

Gaby tried hypnosis, which worked only imperfectly: the man with the cheap look didn't even glance at her, but the other one came round the bar to talk to her.

"Hello Gaby," said this second man; his face was not unpleasant but she didn't believe she knew it. "Don't you recognize me?"

Gaby, stunned, considered him for a moment, then realized she was squinting terribly, damned drink.

"Hmm. Did we ever sleep together?" she fumbled.

"Uhm ... no, I don't think so, no, I'm sure we didn't."

He blushed, young and charming. Okay, it would be this one rather than the other, in life you don't always get your first choice.

"My name is Luc. We talked to each other at Machin Descoteaux last spring, don't you remember?"

As a researcher she talked to fifty thousand two hundred people every year, but this young fellow didn't need to know that, of course.

"Okay," she said, getting up. "But before anything, hungry, very hungry."

"You want to go eat?"

"Yes, eat, yum-yum, lotsa souvlakis pitas at the corner of Saint Joseph."

She left, tipsy and starving; he followed her, laughing, he was hungry too, what a coincidence, and he seemed to find her hilarious, not bad for a start.

They ate. He told her simple things she wasn't sure she entirely understood. She looked at his mouth. He had an eager mouth and carnivorous teeth. When it was time to pay he kindly divided the amount in two and paid only his share, which she found very depressing. Where were the rich and generous men from before feminism, who wrapped their beauteous ladies in rivers of diamonds and made them eat Russian caviar from a teaspoon? Alas. Nothing but fallen romanticism in this almost twenty-first century, nothing but financial ruin.

In the street they walked slowly. He lived in the neighbourhood, wouldn't she like to come to his place for a last drink, see his apartment, listen to Chopin's Opus 59, what do I know, admire his collection of Chinese photographs? Eventually she agreed, after all it was only three in the morning.

Sober now, she watched him out of the corner of her eye, a total stranger, a creature more removed from her than a Zulu from a neo-punk, and in a few minutes they would both be naked and exploring those intimate parts we put so much energy into hiding from others. There was a contradiction there, and more cause for panic than for excitement.

He lived alone in a four-room apartment that resembled

him in every detail: white, impeccably neat, decorated with beautiful objects set out in clinical symmetry. It was like going into a model apartment arranged for prospective buyers, you wanted to look around, then leave. The windows disappeared beneath vertical coal-black blinds, except in the kitchen, where small flowered curtains stood stiffly on guard.

"Did you make the curtains yourself?"

"How did you guess?" he said, surprised.

They sat down on a black sofa that matched the blinds. He offered her a drink. Let's get to it, Gaby wanted to say, but she contented herself with touching his wrist. His reaction was instantaneous: he led her to the bedroom, doubtless to spare the handsome sofa, because love gets things dirty.

He smelled good. His soft skin was like a girl's and his sex admirably aesthetic. Two, three, five times he penetrated her in cadence. After the fifth time she took advantage of a doze—temporary, no doubt, he would be back, would keep going up to twenty at least, these hygienic young men have endurance—to quickly get dressed and flee.

By the time she got home there was light in the sky above Mount Royal. On the doorstep, sitting very respectably on a beautiful pale leather suitcase, Marie-Pierre Deslauriers was waiting for her.

"Hello," said Marie-Pierre Deslauriers as she stood up. "I was wondering if you would agree to offer me your hospitality. Maybe for a day or two."

Gaby showed no surprise. She simply told herself, as she unlocked her apartment door, that it had been an eventful night.

TEN

THIS thing was refusing to work. He pushed *Rewind*, *Stop* and *Record*, anything that might get a reaction, but this arrogant thing, American what's more, didn't move an atom. Dominique Larue cleared his throat professionally, again checked the wires, the plug, the cassette. He allowed a mocking smile to drift across his lips, meanwhile his fingers were shaking. Nothing was working the way he had hoped. Of course he had imagined himself triumphing over the tape recorder with a single glance and coiling with Proustian dignity into an armchair, the aura of the great writers draped over him like an ermine coat. Instead of that, petty problems and grief. And she was about to burst out laughing, he could see her mouth twitching.

"Might I be able to help you?" She offered suavely.

"No, you must be joking!" Dominique laughed. "A writer always has something in his pocket, a pen or a pencil, we'll do without technology, that's all."

He casually punched the tape recorder and sat down in the armchair opposite her. He patted his pockets with an expert smile. He had no pen. Was he going to have to faint or run away screaming? She decided for him, offering him a pad and a felt pen.

"Thank you," Dominique said, "I have an excellent memory but you can never be too careful."

"Never, in fact," She emphasized.

He had succeeded in finding her after agonizing feats. All the radio stations now knew the identity of Dominique Larue, because he had haunted them, one after the other, disturbing the tapings, knocking into technicians in the control rooms, asking his trivial questions of janitors, secretaries and directors alike: he was looking for someone, very certainly a woman, who was said to have pronounced a particular phrase a certain Thursday at about ten o'clock in the morning, wasn't there anyone who could help him? Obviously, if he had thought of writing down the radio frequency he was tuned to things would have been a lot easier, but we can't think of everything when we are in the grip of destiny. (Must the mystic visited by the Celestial Apparition remember the precise form of His ears?... Must the man struck by lightning know if the lightning bolt came from a nimbus cloud or a strato-cumulus?...All right.)

At most of the radio stations he searched out, he was quickly shown the door, but not at CDKP the-city's-most-amusing-radio-station; there he was listened to with great care, then ushered into the office of a researcher who, he was assured, would be better able to answer his questions. At CDKP no one was treated more courteously than the cranks, essential crew to the "Not So Crazy" program and to the ratings. Dominique found himself facing a petite brunette, busy and intimidating, who first looked at him with a vaguely sarcastic friendliness, then with real interest, because by chance he had arrived at the best possible place.

She was not the way he had imagined. Nothing was the way he had imagined. Now he pressed himself into his armchair, waiting for her to speak; this prodigious thing She had experienced was giving him the cold sweats but was tremendously exciting: a transsexual in front of him, with the harsh voice of her fate—that wasn't easy to confront.

"Where do we begin?" She asked.

"Here or there, I mean wherever you want."

A book. He would write a book about her, several, provided that She deigned to furnish him with her secrets, that was the message he'd transmitted to her through the petite sarcastic brunette at whose house, by incredible coincidence, She was living. She had agreed. And what had been only a joke, a useful means of approaching her, evolved inexorably into something else now that She had him in her spell, the old eloquence, the brilliance, the madness was beginning to stir, yes, he would write a fabulous book about her, he would succeed in understanding her, all of her, he would grasp her whole and reveal her soul.

"Hell," Marie-Pierre Deslauriers said abruptly, "is a big dormitory, a gymnasium, a tavern. It's an overwhelming place, hell. Hell has no devil, no fire. Hell is cold, terribly cold."

A long silence. Dominique wondered if She was expecting him to question her, but no questions came to his mind, nothing, he was a passive receptacle that sent back no echo.

"My mother had red hair," She took up in a different voice. "A strength, a heat, she burned everyone who approached her. She was called Aster, which means Star, I never met anyone else whose name was so appropriate. She had conquered all her fears, she was capable of doing anything. She travelled alone, on foot, she could knock off fifty kilometres in a day, and when she was tired she stopped a cart or some car, she hitchhiked before the word was even invented. One day she brought me to the theatre, I was almost six years old; during the intermission the leading actress fell ill and Aster replaced her just like that, at a moment's notice, while they took care of me in the wings. She knew the texts of all the plays by heart, she had a superb voice with modulations that made men turn, she could have become a tragedian, a Québécoise Sarah Bernhardt, or a great opera singer, or even an astronaut if being an astronaut had existed, she was good at everything that requires balance and courage. At sixteen she would climb up to the roofs of buildings, to the tops of bridges, 'to see the entire situation,' she would say. Her laugh. I remember her laugh. Not elegant and artificial like that of other women, no, a storm, something that could shatter windows, an animal explosion. There were always piles of clothes lying around at our house, clothes for laughing, clothes for playing, clothes for being beautiful, she would put them on like a second skin and in two seconds she was someone else. She was a witch, a brush fire. She had thousands of desires, an inexhaustible passion for everything that moved, that was worthy of life. One August the thirteenth at about three in the afternoon, I was twelve years old, I was walking near Mount Royal and I had the very distinct knowledge that she was dead. I knew it without knowing it, from inside, in fact, my body had known it before me and it stopped functioning, I thought I was going to pass out but no, I kept on, a terrible foretaste of unhappiness in my limbs. Unhappiness is such a small word. I could use a cigarette."

Dominique quivered because She was whistling in his direction now, to help herself come back to earth She was addressing herself to him, an almost joyous glow in her look.

"Uhh, I don't smoke," he deplored. "I have no cigarettes."

"I don't smoke either. But I would have one right now, to wrap it all up in a bit of smoke. Too bad."

"I could go get you some, if you like."

"No," She smiled. "Thank you very much. Instead let's see what our friend has hidden in her cupboards. Could you be tempted by a glass of cognac?"

"Yes."

She got up and left the room, he followed her, afraid She wouldn't come back. Her movements were catlike and unpredictable: a chair was in her way, She avoided it by curving her torso like a dancer, She opened the cupboard using only the little finger of her left hand.

"Shit," She grumbled. "I've never met such a junk-food lover."

Under an outrageous heap of bags of chips flavoured with vinegar, ketchup, sour cream and strong spices, She did indeed find a bottle of cognac—empty—and a bottle of Parfait Amour—atrociously mauve.

"I haven't drunk that for at least twenty years," sighed Marie-Pierre, opening the bottle.

"You were in the cradle then...."

She smiled sweetly at the absurd flattery and they went back to the living room.

"Are you managing to follow me without too much difficulty?" She asked.

"Yes," Dominique blushed.

He had written down only one word, in fact, and this with considerable effort: "Aster." The rest was nothing but scribbles, hairy little sketches that the hand traces while the mind is elsewhere.

"I work a lot through impressions," he felt constrained to add.

"Where was I?"

"Your mother."

"No, hell. That's where I was."

She sat down opposite the window, this time taking care not to meet his eyes, and gulped down two glasses of Parfait Amour before recommencing.

"Hell. You don't get used to it, even if it lasts for centuries. When Aster was with me I had already glimpsed it, but in such small quantities, a sort of nasty wink, but Aster was there and no hell could resist her light.

"When she left me there was the terrifying pain of having lost her, but most of all there was the sudden revelation even more frightening, that I was a mistake.

"A mistake everywhere, at every instant of my existence. I wasn't only alone, which would have been ordinary and perhaps almost bearable; I was monstrous, and I atoned for this monstrousness constantly, at every second, except at night when I slept; when I was able to sleep, after having cried, vomited and peed in my bed because of the anxiety and incomprehension.

"Since Aster's death I had been a boarder in a school. A boys' school, of course, because it was obvious to everyone that I was a boy. There was only me—and Aster—to know.

"I don't know how to explain it. Even today, after having to convince so many people so many times, I don't know how to find the right words, the words to make things clear once and for all, so people would say *so that's how it is*. Maybe such words don't exist.

"I had a boy's body, you see, with a phallus, sprouting hairs, everything, but inside I was a girl, I KNEW I was a girl. It was a certainty that went back to the beginning, to the first stirrings of my consciousness, perhaps to the womb, it was an unshakeable certainty.

"It's impossible, they say. Nature can't make this kind of mistake. Nevertheless nature is always playing tricks. There are people born with three arms, a horse's head, missing chromosomes, there are deformed animals and vegetables, there are all those errors we don't know about because they are hidden away in people's heads. Where exactly, in precisely which brain cells, are the sexual identities of people imprinted? Do you know?…. I don't, yet I desperately tried to find out. I was a great scientist, I searched through the infinitely tiny. What makes us KNOW we are a man or a woman, physical attributes aside? Why are you yourself so persuaded that you're a man? If only I could answer those questions which have no answers. Before my operation the psychiatrists pressed me to furnish them with irrefutable proof: 'What are you feeling?… What is a woman?… Are you aggressive?… Do you like money?… Might you not be, instead, a homosexual who's denying it? Draw me a sheep, a giraffe, a teeter-totter. Do you like sex?'

"But I'm digressing. That was after. Before there were those years of school, that daily atrocity.

"Nothing but boys all around, and male professors who sensed my difference without being able to put their fingers on it, and who hated me for that, nothing but male sports and the necessity to behave like a man, so much noise in the dormitories, and violent games, and rigid thoughts that weren't mine…. An accumulation of small terrible things that sometimes turned into unusually spectacular events— like that time some boys forced me to swallow urine, or other times when a teacher forced me to masturbate him, or those times I was called 'fag bastard,' and the beatings I got during—what a sinister name—recreation periods. But the worst was within me, a perpetual terror, the feeling of being a living failure, a lie, to have gotten lost among extraterrestials, to be wandering around at a vampire ball. For me, hell is exactly that: a masquerade that never ends, a werewolf costume you can't take off.

"And yet I liked dressing in costumes when Aster was there: but it was as MYSELF that I always dressed, a serious little girl who knows she is illicit."

"How did Aster die?"

She turned towards Dominique, flabbergasted that he had spoken, or perhaps even that he still existed, She had been talking with her innermost self, and her blurred reflection in the window.

"Didn't I tell you? She drowned."

"Excuse me. Please keep going."

"No. That's enough for today."

Shaken, Dominique understood that She was telling him to leave, but he had no desire to leave, he was suspended amid the stirred-up fragments of his life; if he let them go he might be swallowed by the void.

"All right. Will I see you tomorrow?"

"No. Next week, or the week after. Call me. I'll see."

So long. How to survive such a wait? She got up, inflexible. He got up too, stoic.

"Your father," he said hesitantly, "you haven't told me about your father."

She stared at him unblinking; he had the feeling that a sort of infrared was going through his insides, down to the marrow of his bones. He blushed.

"He was dead when I was born. I never met him. There's nothing to say about my father. And yours, how is he?"

•

"Sick. He's gone into the hospital."

It was about six in the evening, Mado was waiting for him at the door, upset at the prospect of upsetting him, nonetheless overexcited by this authentic first, perhaps a bump on the smooth road of their love, but at least something new.

"Your father, Maurice.... Very sick. The doctor called."

She carefully repeated herself while watching him out of the corner of her eye, because Dominique was slow to show anything, even stunned surprise; then he decided to react, but badly—he started to laugh.

"Excuse me," he said. "I'm laughing because. What's the name of the hospital."

"I'll come with you."

"No."

She looked hurt and resigned, she who would have liked to know everything about his sorrows in fact knew nothing, but if I bring you to see my father, my sweet, the old devil will take pleasure in letting you know how I use my Thursday mornings that are costing you so much, and you will know how treacherous and dishonest I am and your feelings will be hurt.

"I'd prefer to see him alone," he added soberly.

"I understand," she said with infinite tenderness.

The old devil was sitting up in his bed. Dominique didn't go in right away, his spine was frozen with fear. Cancer, the doctor had said, cancer cancer cancer, and Dominique had distinctly seen them crawling, those aggressive little beasts that hack and tear apart and attack human life.

Maurice was sulking. He was refusing the hospital food

and medications, he refused to speak to anyone, he had refused to let them inform his son, but the doctor had become outraged, exasperated by Maurice's infantile stubbornness. "Your father is denying his illness," the doctor had told Dominique, to which Dominique had replied that he could hardly be blamed for that.

"What are you doing here?" Maurice said sharply. "It's not Thursday."

"I know."

"Is that imbecile the one who phoned you? Tell me."

"Uhh....yes. Yes."

"Imbecile," Maurice sneered. "All imbeciles, you most of all. You come running here like an imbecile. I'm getting out tomorrow morning."

"Not tomorrow morning, Papa. In a few days, maybe."

"I'M GETTING OUT TOMORROW MORNING."

Dominique sat down opposite the bed. It was a double room, chalky white, populated by persistent odours—the odours of illness and disinfectants twined together, it was hard to know which was stronger and more unbearable. Maurice's bed was next to the window. The other bed was unoccupied. Maurice's face had grown still thinner, as though sucked away from the inside, only his eyes retained an angry spark of colour.

"It's good that you're near a window," Dominique said. "It's snowing, look, the first snow."

"Cut it out. They've mixed me up with someone else, they want to treat me for diseases I don't have. IMBECILES. I want to get out of here, the sheets are filthy."

His father's hand came and went on the impeccably white sheet and Dominique, fascinated, followed its movements, trembling and ethereal, strange strange he could not help comparing this hand to that of Marie-Pierre Deslauriers, the same feathery agitation, the same graceful way of slowly unfolding and straightening his fingers, strange and ludicrous.

"I'm going to let myself die of hunger," Maurice said.

"Papa, no."

"Yes. Stop contradicting me. Get me out of here."

Suddenly he let out an agitated whimper and curled up in his bed; a sharp pain had just passed through his stomach. Dominique looked at him without saying a word.

"I'm sick," Maurice said, and began to sob silently.

Get up, sit on the bed, take Maurice's shivering hands into his own, poor absurd distant relatives of Marie-Pierre's hands, whose memory still moved him, touch Maurice for once, but it wasn't possible, years of ice had done their damage.

"Would you like anything?" Dominique asked, his voice neutral. "What can I do for you?"

"Take me with you."

And since Dominique made no reply, Maurice turned on his side, towards the window, permanently banished to himself.

"You see?" he murmured. "No one can help anyone else."

ELEVEN

HER father had put on a breathtaking dress, one of those that dared to be as low in front as behind, enough to make the viewer cross-eyed. Her father was very beautiful tonight.

Camille was proud to see she was not alone in her opinion: the whole restaurant had yielded to her father's charm. Five times already, the headwaiter had come to inquire after the ladies' well-being, a saccharine smile on his lips. And the men at the neighbouring tables, although accompanied by their legitimate females, kept peering in their direction, magnetized by her father's low neckline and the long white limb casually emerging from the slit in her father's dress.

"He's looking at you again. The other one too. And the fat bearded one at the back has moved his chair just so you'll be in his field of vision."

"And now what are they doing?" her father asked, wriggling his back so that his dress would move farther up his thigh.

"Now," Camille almost choked on her crayfish, "they can't stand it anymore. The fat bearded guy has put on his glasses, the little skinny one has stopped chewing, the other is stabbing the table with his fork...."

"Let's hope they don't eat their ties."

Laughter, laughter.

The champagne was rebelliously tickling Camille's brain. She was drinking it in huge clandestine gulps whenever the waiter and the headwaiter deigned to look elsewhere, which didn't happen very often. For three weeks she and her father had been "doing" the best restaurants. Camille now knew that she didn't like caviar or oysters, but that marrow fritters, goose liver with truffles, and anything with morels or crayfish were delicacies guaranteed to make her feel wonderful.

"Might the ladies desire a light sweet to amuse their taste buds?"

The waiter had come back to haunt their table, his slender silhouette bent over Marie-Pierre's corsage, his expression soft and paternal. An endive, thought Camille, who had just tried one for the first time in her life and hadn't really liked it.

"What do you think, Hhhilda?" asked Marie-Pierre, her eyebrow raised several inchs.

"Uhh…uhh…" Camille stammered, seized with the giggles.

"My daughter will have another goose pâté. With a small dab of whipped cream on the side."

"The…with the…?" the waiter babbled.

"That is what you want, Hhhilda?"

"Yes M-m-other," Camille mumbled into her napkin.

"Good. And for me a triple Armagnac, period. My taste buds are sufficiently amused."

She sent him away with a smile that allowed no reply. Camille chuckled softly. These Wednesday evenings had turned out to be incredibly pleasurable parties that nourished the rest of her week with dreams and wild laughter. Her father would dress up in one of the two audacious outfits he owned, to provide a distraction; as for Camille, she dressed as she could—as, to be exact, Michèle permitted—that is to say, in an invariable strict little suit that at least had the advantage of showing she came from a good family. Groomed and proper, they would slip into those luxurious establishments where the least little bowl of soup costs you fifteen dollars, and there they would gobble and laugh and misbehave in public under the benevolent eye of the restaurateur, because money is a grand master in this minuscule existence. Of money they had none, but the benevolent restaurateur didn't have to know that.

Her father was always in brilliant form. He adorned her with pointed and hilarious names (Cunegonde, Myrtillette, Josephasse) to which she replied with giggling servility (yes, M-m-mother, very well, M-m-mother); with her he invented impossible languages that made the waiters' ears turn—discreetly—towards them.

"*That*-de-duh *wai*-de-do *ter*-de-dow *is*-de-di *an*-de-day *id*-de-die *iot*-de-dum."

"*Yes*-de-dor. *Stu*-de-doo *pid*-de-did *and*-de-die *bo*-day *ring*-de-dum."

She drank champagne. She ate complex and sophisticated dishes. In her father's made-up eyes she saw the glow of a joyous tenderness that satisfied her stomach as much as a duck confit or a slice of guinea hen. She sucked on parsley before going home, barely wavering on her feet, so that no trace of champagne would be discernible to Michèle's distrustful nose, Michèle who thought they were eating at some McDonald's.

The M moment arrived. M for Mystification and Monopoly. The waiter presented Marie-Pierre with the bill, along with some of the house sweets and an additional

Armagnac courtesy of the headwaiter. Marie-Pierre thanked him with a princely batting of her eyelashes, too kind, my good friend.

"This all seems very reasonable," she simpered over the bill. "Doesn't it, Hhhilda?"

"Yes, M-m-other. Indeed, much less expensive than at Halle...."

The total was astronomical: $398. Infinitely more than Marie-Pierre spent in order to survive innumerable weeks.

"Could you calculate the little fifteen per cent tip, my dear?"

"Of c-course." Camille closed her eyes for a fraction of a second: fifteen per cent of three hundred and ninety-eight, I keep back four, I keep back four....Fifty-nine dollars and sixty, no, seventy cents, excuse me."

Her father contemplated her for a moment with a very real deference.

"Shit," he murmured, "that's what I call a quick mind."

"But Papa, that's nothing," Camille couldn't help saying. "I can usually calculate more complicated things in my head much faster. When I'm sober,..." she finished, giggling.

"Damned quick," Marie-Pierre repeated, this time with a touch of worry in her look.

Then Camille, still giggling, watched her father take out his wallet and, from his wallet, a large number of bills. She watched him lean forward and spread his legs following a subtle procedure whose efficacity had been memorably established, she watched everyone's eyes converge on the white flesh thus exposed and linger there, oblivious of all else, which was the goal of the operation. Because in the wad of papers Marie-Pierre had just slid under the bill there were a few Canadian dollars—for the pleasing face and symbol of the queen—and a quantity of phony bills—for their thickness.

What followed was a question of velocity, and depended on the necessary grace period good restaurants wait before sticking their noses in your money. Trailing smiles and promises to return and along with fulsome congratulations to the chef and emotional swayings of the posterior, it was necessary to escape without seeming to—and before the waiter was introduced to the Monopoly and Canadian Tire bills. Once at the door, it was necessary to run.

They ran. Marie-Pierre held her slippers in her hands like a supersonic Cinderella, and while they ran they laughed and howled like crazy people, inventing complicated routes to shake off hypothetical pursuers. In truth these Wednesday evenings were bits of raw, barbaric happiness with no bad aftertaste, just the ferocious desire to continue to transgress in order to live.

They went down Saint-Denis arm in arm. It was a moment of perfect serenity. Camille floated blissfully, absurdly happy. She loved her father's odour, which was filtering into her nostrils; the first signs of Christmas brightening up the store windows; the small icy clouds exhaled from people's mouths. Everyone they encountered became an islet of fraternal warmth at whom she had an irresistible desire to smile. Marie-Pierre seemed to be gripped by a similar mood. She was walking slowly, her step light, she too was smiling at everyone, especially the men, and then gradually Camille saw her father's eyes and smile beginning to fill with that languid glow she didn't like. It signified that she was no longer enough, and it arrived, inevitably, at the end of their evenings together. A frenzy from which she was excluded began to take over her father—this father who was now entirely a woman—who was walking beside her like a stranger, transformed by a desire that bordered on pain.

"It's getting late, isn't it, my treasure?"

"No," Camille said sullenly.

"Yes, it's getting late. You get up early tomorrow. And me too."

"NO!"

"I'll take you back to Berri-de-Montigny. Aren't you cold in that little knit jacket?"

Camille began to panic and hung onto his arm.

"Please, let's stay for a while, PLEASE!"

"Be reasonable," Marie-Pierre sighed, brazenly returning the look of a passerby.

"I don't want to go back," Camille howled. "Please, Daddy, DADDY!"

Marie-Pierre made a face, glanced quickly around. Camille took this opportunity to step up her vehemence, while heads turned and people stared in astonishment at the two women.

"DADDY!"

"Sshhh."

"Please, DADDY! DADDY!"

Marie-Pierre stopped short and took her by the shoulders.

"Listen," she whispered icily. "Either you shut up right away and you go back to the house or you never see me again, NEVER, do you hear me?"

"Nasty," Camille mumbled.

But, defeated, she stayed quiet.

She refused Marie-Pierre's arm as they walked to the subway, refused any display of emotion, went through the door with her eyes obstinately riveted to the ground. But as she was about to be swallowed up by the stairway, walled into her total despair, something overcame her and she turned towards her father still waiting on the other side of the door, oh that loving and heartbreaking smile of his, "Until Wednesday, until Wednesday," he silently mouthed and Camille's resentment instantly evaporated, she waved her hand frantically and blew him dozens of kisses, don't forget me think of me Daddy—the subway passengers must have thought she was a bit crazy but she could not have cared less.

Couples. Couplings. Human beings function in couples, bound two by two to their brief destinies as bipeds, there seemed to be an inexorable law that said this was proper and should be perpetuated. Even her father, for all the laws he transgressed, did not escape this one. The need for another body to attach oneself to. Would she necessarily follow the same course? Were there no exceptions? How could she believe that the shrivelled gentleman kneading his eyebrows opposite her, the pimply adolescents who were secretly smoking at her side, the subway conductor, the various people hanging about the stations and even this enormous Asian lugging parcels as big as herself all had SOMEONE joined to their lives, or aspired to join themselves to someone?

Camille curled up on the seat of the subway, suddenly brought to earth by the evidence: yes, everything in the universe functioned in couples, beginning with those double stars that orbited each other and alternately masked each other's light. Beginning, above all, with that most perfect image of blending together—those terrifying couples whose intimacy was a product of the most fantastic paradox: black holes and quasars.

She loved black holes. She loved the fact that they existed and defied human understanding.

Black holes are dead stars, the cores of exploded stars that have collapsed into themselves, so compressed and turned inwards that the entire matter of the star is now contained within a ridiculously tiny space of infinite density. So go understand that. The infinite density means that nothing more will escape this dead star, not even light, so this dead star will become invisible forever, and those on earth who aim their fat telescopic eyes at it will find nothing, zilch. But there are crazier things than that. What makes quasars, the most luminous things in the universe, shine so brightly? Black holes—imagine.

Puzzled, astronomers discovered that quasars, terribly far away, couldn't be simple stars: at such considerable distances no star could display these excesses of energy. Still just as puzzled, these same astronomers—or maybe others—bet that quasars were the cores of abnormally bright galaxies. Abnormally, because the quasars were found next to black holes, how interesting, and such close proximity cannot lead to normal phenomena.

Thus the action takes place in the core of galaxies: that is where black holes are most likely to form, because of the strong concentration of stars and, *a posteriori*, the cadavers of stars. So what happens when a massive black hole develops at the heart of a galaxy? It sucks up whatever gravitates to it. Gaseous particles, stars of every type, whatever gravitates to it abruptly falls, blazing, into the black hole. The swan song of the matter spinning and flaming around a black hole before being swallowed up—that's a quasar.

What happens afterwards, in the black hole, is unknowable and no longer belongs to the physical universe.

The universe's most luminous entity suddenly twinned to its darkest, all fates mixed up, all paradoxes levelled: that was the true marvel. Could we not find a sort of reassuring symbolism there, a metaphor glorifying the fusion of opposites?

Monk Station. Camille decided to walk home from there; the champagne bubbles seemed to have become solid and were sitting like stones in her stomach. She thought about Lucky Poitras, her exact antonym, more quasar than black hole, because of the light, but dragging her into a magnetic abyss, she who didn't blaze and who magnetized no one and who decidedly had nothing in common with any of these galactic marvels. The comparison turned out to be limp; better to leave stars and humans to their respective fates.

Human beings are so fragile....

"I pay attention, I swear, I always try to talk to her nicely—"

"I was referring to you," said J. Boulet.

"Oh?" Michèle blushed, and she made a hasty retreat behind her coffee cup.

"You aren't happy, Michèle... may I call you Michèle?"

He continued to weigh her down with the serious look of those who know and empathize. It made her feel upset and distraught, no one had talked to her this way for centuries—and what clairvoyance, he knew things about her she hadn't even suspected.

"Of course," she sighed, "life isn't ... often isn't easy."

She had to stop because of the tears filling her respiratory passages, a deluge. J. Boulet stretched a hand out towards her, but it stopped just short of her wrist, as though held back by respect.

"Go ahead, let yourself go, go ahead, I understand you, yes, cry...."

Michèle sobbed, lulled by the approving gentleness of this voice; it was only when she unexpectedly saw herself in the living-room mirror that she asked herself what she was doing there, crumpled like a dishcloth by the side of an almost stranger, her hair in her face and her body very unaesthetically broken in two, she was going to ruin her silk dress and moreover, gadzooks, why was she blubbering like this? She immediately straightened up with great dignity.

"Excuse me." She blew her nose.

"No..."

"Yes."

He followed her into the kitchen with their two coffee cups, which he began to rinse meticulously.

"Leave that."

"No...."

"Yes."

Their hands collided above the sink; they hurriedly pulled them back with perfect synchronization and a small frightened laugh.

"I should leave," J. Boulet ventured. "Your daughter will be back soon."

"No. She always comes home very late when she goes out with her...father."

She sighed, J. Boulet nodded his head sorrowfully, they sat down side by side, and without consulting each other, on the stools next to the counter. The main part of the conversation had been about Camille, of course. She was piling up failure after failure, especially in science and mathematics, she could no longer stand it when teachers talked to her in public, she seemed to be pathologically antisocial, without friends or confidants, went from class to class like a mute ghost, neither inattentive nor talkative during lectures, no, in fact she had an icy concentration, never lowering her head to take notes, subjecting the teachers to a constant surveillance that upset them because they felt it was a kind of swaggering and arrogance.... J. Boulet had no solution, he was simply allowing himself to share his perplexity with Michèle—whom he had already met once for similar reasons—and he dared to present a hypothesis, neurosis, yes, perhaps we might speak of a neurosis, still benign, let's not panic.

"I'm very worried."

"It's not easy, I understand...."

"I'm very afraid of him, you know, but at the same time, at the same time..."

"Yes, I understand your hesitation."

".... he's...he's a pathetic character, and it seems that in a way he's good for Camille, just for now, of course..."

"Of course, you also have to take the longer view, look at the consequences ..."

"He's dangerous for sensitive types.... he's extremely intelligent, you know.... Dangerously...."

"People who are too intelligent are always dangerous."

"To me, in any case—he's already...hurt me a lot."

"I know, Michèle."

She raised her eyes, misted over with gratitude; spontaneously he took her hand, then immediately let go of it, before she quite realized what he'd done.

"Do you have children?" she asked nervously.

"Yes and no. I have none and I have two thousand...."

"Yes, of course, a comprehensive high school, what a terrible responsibility ..."

"...which yields great joy, also. VERY great, believe me," he insisted vehemently.

"I believe you."

He got up, his eyes filled with a swampy sadness. Michèle asked herself if there was something offensive in what she had said or omitted to say, found no answer, and in the spirit of solidarity she got up too. An uncomfortable silence.

"I haven't had occasion to procreate."

"Ah,..." Michèle said cautiously.

"No. To bring children into the world, for me, constitutes an act of love, of...of love, yes, let's not be afraid of words, no doubt I am old-fashioned."

"Oh no...."

"Oh yes. Love did not arrive," he concluded, his voice knotted by adversity.

Michèle felt relieved; for a moment she had thought he must have problems with fertility or impotence, and that possibility, she had to admit, would have annoyed her.

"Ah!... Love!..." she exhaled painfully.

"Yes, love!... And loneliness!"

"Ah!... Loneliness!...."

They exchanged smiles of distress and, without exactly knowing how, found themselves excessively close to each other, trying to kiss across their clinking teeth.

Outside, Camille, who was watching them through the window, smiled wickedly; the battle would be easier, now that her enemies had joined forces in the same camp.

TWELVE

H E was undressing her. In slow motion that erased one button at a time, lingered over the zipper, exposed a beginning of shoulder, skin sliding out of the cloth in a slow progression, imperceptible yet sure of itself. A liturgy, let us say.

Finally the dress slipped off.

Next he started on her stockings, inciting them to slide towards her feet with immense slowness, every millimetre of skin thus visited came abruptly into the world and began to shiver. Panties and brassiere: his hands ignored their existence for the moment, were content to treat them as a second skin, to be touched lightly or massaged for the joy of the contrast. He turned her all around, touched her everywhere without insisting, she was dizzy with expectation, what came next was bound to be powerful.

He tore off the rest of her clothes, ripping them in half, left her there for a few seconds, completely naked and vulnerable. He looked at her. All this in complete silence. Then he pushed her onto the bed, she was touched all over, spread apart, sucked, licked and sanctified, an object, perhaps, but the object of an explosive cult, again and again she came, crying out, she came as we are born, into a void that is always beginning.

"Get undressed. Quickly. I want to see them."

Marie-Pierre looked at him, flabbergasted. He was already sitting naked on the bed, his sex erect and ready for action. He was talking to her. What was he saying?

"Come on! Take off your clothes!"

She started to unbutton her dress. But her heart wasn't in it, this guy wouldn't stop talking and that made it difficult for her to concentrate. The hardest thing was imagining herself elsewhere, in a marble room with Ionic columns and Egyptian servants fanning her with large eucalyptus leaves, for example, with someone distinguished and silent opposite her, above all neither nude nor pot-bellied nor sexual, to tell the truth, like this man, my God, reality can be so disappointing.

"Show them to me. Come here so I can—"

"Shut your face," Marie-Pierre grunted, buttoning herself back up.

Too bad, it wouldn't be this time either, there are limits to be respected or the dream collapses. Of course given her fantasies, this idea of following anything with hair into its cave did lead to a few disagreements.

"What are you doing?"

The man stood up. He seemed discontent, no doubt he had been expecting something.

"Listen, this is boring me, so I'm on my way. See you!"

"What? What do you mean, 'see you'—slut!"

First the swearwords, then the battle, all right, he wanted to kiss her, to hold her against his sexual excrescence and his heart, all right, all right, by force, naturally, that's what they prefer, the little ladies. Marie-Pierre pushed him away, hard, but the leech wouldn't let go so she regretfully gave him a knee in the stomach, which left him folded up and green. *If you can't fuck them, hit them.* But she shouldn't get into the habit, it tended to take away the romance.

Lost in black thoughts, she took a taxi back to Gaby's. Life was turning out to be dull. When would the exceptional being arrive at her side to discover her, to take her, to move her entrails and take her virginity, God, where were the REAL MEN hiding?

THIRTEEN

HERE was something new in Gaby's life. To the point that she no longer recognized herself: mirrors reflected the image of a girl with bright curious eyes and a perpetually serene smile; the bags of chips were in danger of rotting away in her cupboards.

On the one hand, she was in love. Oh yes. This inoffensive young dandy with the name of Luc had vanquished her resistance, her, the armoured one, the more-than-immunized. And he had gone about it in the most conventional way there is, the animal. Patience and seduction.

He had telephoned her a few days after their innocuous night. Ring-ring.

"Yes?" Gaby had answered, succinct, because she was at CDKP, battling a madwoman who claimed to be telepathically connected to birds and wanted at all costs to be on Bob Mireau's program.

"It's me, Luc."

"Who?"

"I would like to apologize for the other night."

"Poor poor turkeys," said the madwoman. "We don't realize what great anguish ..."

"Why?" Gaby resumed.

"Because of CHRISTMAS, all that business!... The turkeys in the ovens, the cranberry ..."

"Because I'm afraid I was a bit hasty ..."

"Oh no," Gaby said weakly.

"Oh yes," he said.

"Yes!" screamed the birdophile. "A MASSACRE of turkeys and capons in the holiday season! We are ASSASSINS!"

And so on and so forth for hours, perhaps, had Gaby wanted to get involved in misunderstandings and silly games, but she quickly got rid of the madwoman by booting her out of her office, and then she prepared to do the same with the other.

"Give me another chance," he pleaded.

So be it, my little chick. Besides, the competition wasn't beating the door down; Gaby's libidinous life was a desert, and only Gudule the spider watched over her insomnia. He invited her to supper at his place that evening.

"Late," Gaby warned him. "I have an insane amount of work."

"Whenever's best for you is good for me."

She arrived at his place at about midnight.

He must have been disappointed, but he didn't show it. On the other hand, the bird he'd proposed to feed her had not lasted so well, and lay stiffly in the bottom of a baking dish.

"It was a duck," he explained.

"Poor thing."

They sucked on a few calcified bones and ate some vegetables. This Luc had, in fact, a great intellectual and practical mastery of vegetables. He knew all sorts of touching things about them—that the colours green and bright yellow are a guaranteed index of a high amount of carotene, that the beneficial fibres and mineral salts are in the skins, that steaming preserves the most vitamins and that the daily consumption of raw cruciferous plants wards off cancer, mononucleosis and other bodily disasters. Gaby listened to him with a kind of awe. She was used to a flow of conversation that was showy and unpredictable; at CDKP, quite aside from the nuts who forcefully led you into their untracked imaginations, there was a continuous barrage of crackling comments on the gaffes of this minister, the sexual anatomy of another, a mishmash of childishness and playfulness leaving your head empty but your heart incapable of boredom. And suddenly this demented discourse. The brassica family includes broccoli, Brussels sprouts, cabbage, cauliflower, kohlrabi, rutabaga and turnips, and they should be eaten several times a week. In order to preserve your health. Therefore there was, somewhere, a health to preserve, strange strange, how had this Luc come to penetrate such mysteries?

Looking at him more closely, everything in him exuded sanity and health. He had never smoked and drank only moderately; he took care of his body, which paid him back splendidly. Fresh breath, shining eyes, silky skin, responsive muscles. Seventy lengths of an Olympic pool twice a week. A hundred sit-ups every morning. Cross-country skiing and canoe-camping trips in the appropriate seasons. Healthy food, lots of spring water, all-out war against bulge-making lipids and overexciting glucose. When he offered her dessert—a kiwi-and-unflavoured-yogurt parfait—Gaby could only eat it respectfully, penetrated by the conviction that she was eating vast portions of eternal health.

And kind, so kind.

He brought her things, he took them away. The moment the plates were empty they were instantly returned, without her doing a thing, to the cupboard and the cleanliness from which they had doubtless never entirely departed, there were flowers on the table, mimosa and three tropical roses, when she said her neck was stiff he massaged it for a few moments, he put on some Chopin studies brilliantly interpreted by Louis Lortie and she began to feel peaceful and harmonious, so kind, he always left the toilet seat down in the women's position because he had been brought up in a family of daughters, feminist and so kind, he read Elizabeth Badinter and Marie Cardinal and didn't understand why the country wasn't run by a woman, he fixed her a bubble bath scented with green apple, which restores the skin and tones the body, she slid into it and fell asleep right away, a vague foetal smile on her lips.

She woke up at eight in the morning. He had put her to bed and tucked her in. Perhaps he had even watched over her all night, because as soon as she woke up she saw him looking at her, hazel eyes bright and vigilant. She crawled to his chest, sank into it and purred, which is why they didn't even make love, she fell asleep again in this inconceivable warmth and she dreamt easy, playful dreams, the bad people had died, she was small again and being cradled in the arms of her father and mother together.

She saw him again the next day. Luc Desautels, he was called. Despite the terrible weather—icy enough for the worst nightmares of the uni-legged, with humidity that pierced to the marrow—he had come to wait for her at the CDKP exit. Look, he attacked, the situation seemed simple to him: she was free, so was he, he found her attractive, she seemed not indifferent to him. Why not try something together?... She was disarmed by his frankness and the solidity of his logic, and could find no intelligent argument.

That night they embraced with a new excitement that augured well for the future. Her old kleptomania moved to tears, Gaby took a silk scarf—a red Hermès decorated with sketched warriors—and he didn't notice.

That was how it all began, in a tangle of the stunning trivialities that make love so difficult to forget. I want to take care of you, he told her. You are beautiful. Kind. Funny. So much so. I love your eyes, your breasts, the lines starting to form on your face. I love the way your stomach rumbles.

While making love to her he nibbled her ear lobes. He bought her a steamer, a pressure cooker and recipe books on how to prepare vegetables. Once, at his place, he said, "I think I love you."

And another time, in her bedroom, he said, "Oh! A spider!"

Gaby hardly had time to react before Gudule had been crushed against the wall, green and red and very dead. But that took its place in the order of things; passion cannot be born without victims.

On the other hand, Marie-Pierre Deslauriers. Since the fateful night when she had occupied Gaby's apartment, she seemed to have no inclination to move on. The most amazing thing was that Gaby didn't really mind—in fact she felt a sort of unconditional attraction: something that was less sympathy than a tremendous curiosity led her to desire the presence of the transsexual.

And she had found the means, very prosaic, of extending Marie-Pierre's stay at her place. She stocked her refrigerator with red meats. With beef, bourgeois and distinguished, that she heroically procured at Anjou Québec, where they do not skimp on other people's money. Marie-Pierre had a passionate love for meat. It was not unusual to surprise her at three in the morning leaning against the kitchen table, her eyes filled with lust, chewing away at a half-raw filet mignon. All these animal proteins cost extravagant sums which she was not in a position to reimburse. After devouring pounds and pounds of tartares, fondues, chateaubriands, bavettes and other precious red delicacies, graciously furnished by her hostess, she was gripped by a scruple, and one morning she spoke of it to Gaby.

"As a way of returning the favour," she suggested, "I will give your house a thorough cleaning. I will clean like a BULL!"

She was going to repaint the apartment, clean and scour the closets, put Gaby's summer clothes into storage after soaking them in super-soft water and non-alkaline soaps, wash the windows until they shone, clean the carpets, scald the dishes that weren't being used, in brief, hunt down every last speck of dust. Gaby didn't refuse; she hardly had the time to devote herself to the duster and the vacuum, and obscure social anxieties had always kept her from taking advantage of the services, even paid, of a housekeeper.

Gaby went to spend the weekend in Luc's bed; when she came back forty-eight hours later, still tangled in the sulphurous vapours of her debauchery, nuclear war had broken out in her apartment, the sky had fallen to earth or vice versa, in sum there had been a cataclysm. Everything normally hidden in the cupboards or in storage was spread out on the floor; Gaby's innumerable possessions had occupied the territory and were, it seemed to her, laughing triumphantly; the couches were leaning on the beds and the carpets had been rolled up. It looked like the aftermath of some Devil's sabbath—priests and bishops would have to be summoned so the place could be exorcized.

She finally found Marie-Pierre cornered behind the television, haggard and overwhelmed, emptying a bottle of Parfait Amour.

"What a pain," Marie-Pierre grimaced in her direction. "Housecleaning gives me a pain. What joy could a liberated woman find in that, can you tell me?…"

Gaby solved the problem by hiring maintenance men, a whole team of them, who spared no sarcastic remark while straightening out the mess and charging her the sun and the moon. The two never discussed cleaning again.

But despite her guest's inability to make herself useful, Gaby continued to manoeuvre to keep her at her place. Professional deformation, perhaps; morbid fascination with the marginal and sensational—she felt compelled to scrutinize, though trying to appear not to, the transsexual's every gesture.

This woman had been a man; therefore, somewhere beneath those chemically and surgically constructed curves, a man must still exist, silenced but real: how could she resist searching for his traces, resist carefully watching this being who dared, in broad daylight, to contain the two great contradictions of the human race? Gaby began observing Marie-Pierre whenever she could, indirectly but very closely, for who knows, the key to this living enigma might be lost in the blink of an eyelash. Marie-Pierre acted as though she didn't know she was being watched, until one day she put her cards on the table.

"I don't care if you look at me, my dear," she said calmly. "I like being looked at. But do it openly, it makes me sick when people try to stare at me without seeming to."

So Gaby was forced, right there, to admit she had a certain propensity for voyeurism. Meanwhile, it quickly became apparent that Marie-Pierre had nothing against exhibitionism. She ostentatiously put on her makeup and manicured herself in the living room, she tried on clothes and flimsy undergarments in front of the tall mirror in the dining room, she left the door wide open when she was taking a bath or undressing...Gradually, Gaby stopped hypocritically turning her eyes away, and between them a strange and peculiar relationship was established: one revelling in continuous performance, the other in the perverse passivity of the spectator who knows she is the entire audience.

Someone else was magnetized by Marie-Pierre Deslauriers, no doubt for different reasons, and he made no secret of it. He would burst into the apartment at unlikely hours, usually finding no one but Gaby, because Marie-Pierre was often away for long periods. He was a writer, according to what Gaby could remember from their first hurried encounter at CDKP; his writings were still meagre—she wasn't familiar with his name or anything he'd done—he said he wanted to further his work on the back of Marie-Pierre (a manner of speaking, because he was obviously greatly and painfully fascinated by ALL of Marie-Pierre's anatomy).

He brought neither tape recorder nor notepad; just gloves, sometimes, and an alert curiosity which made him look both disturbed and malicious. Usually he knocked, asked whether Marie-Pierre was there, expressed a brief and polite regret, then left right away. Once Gaby invited him in for coffee and he accepted.

They sat in the kitchen. He would actually prefer a glass of water with a bit of lemon, if that wasn't inconvenient, ah, she had no lemon, so he would have coffee.

"You must find me tiring," he said, looking away from her.

"Persevering, let's say."

"She isn't often here."

"Yes, she goes out."

"Where does she go?"

He bit his cheeks right away, aware that his curiosity was beyond the normal bounds, and without blinking he gulped down half his steaming coffee.

"Where does she go?" he insisted, a little more weakly.

"The Devil knows," Gaby hissed, comically lugubrious, but the Author didn't laugh, he was content to stare wide-eyed with obvious worry. "Not very far," she added, seized by compassion. "She likes to walk."

"To walk."

"Yes."

"I like walking too. I walk every day on my way back from the hospital. Your apartment is on my way."

"You work in a hospital?"

"No. My father has been hospitalized. Cancer all over."

That kind of repartee shoots down your jokes in full flight; how can you go on to exchange pleasantries about life, death and all those things? But he gave her a disconcerting and furtive smile that meant—*don't worry, let's forget all that*—and she started to like him, he wasn't so bad after all, except for his habit of chewing his cheeks at the slightest provocation, as though his various anxieties wouldn't stop attacking him.

"How is your book going?"

"Which one?"

"The one you're writing. Aren't you writing a book?"

"Yes, yes," he blushed. "It's coming, it's coming, I promise. In my mind it's almost done."

She couldn't keep back a loud untimely laugh, he joined her without protest and they clinked their cups of coffee together like old tavern buddies.

"I really envy you," he said suddenly.

"Why?"

"You live with her. You see everything, or almost. What excites her, what interests her, what she likes, what she reads, how she eats...."

"Like a glutton. That's how she eats. Are you in love with her?"

"Yes. I don't know. Worse than that, I'm afraid. Sometimes I'd like to trade places with her mirror."

She looked into mirrors a lot. Before going to sleep, before going out in the evening for one of those mysterious walks. That smug way she had of looking at herself. And those unbelievable dresses, clinging, cut low for all to see, breast-displayers more than anything else. When a glimmer of disapproval showed in Gaby's eye, Marie-Pierre noticed immediately even though she was absorbed in her reflection.

"Don't you like my dress?" she asked smoothly.

"Hmmm. A bit obscene."

"What do you mean, obscene? But all women, my little kitten, LOVE their breasts to be noticed. You yourself, for example, your blouse is a bit transparent and you're not wearing a bra, and that dress you put on to show off your figure .... Now don't contradict me. That roundabout way you have, you biological women, of showing yourselves off while seeming to do the opposite, all right, YES, I show off my breasts, and proudly if you want to know, look how beautiful they are. Hypocrisy, that's what's obscene."

She said that, Marie-Pierre, and then she went out, in her gorgeous and daring low-cut dress.

Afterwards Gaby spent a long moment studying herself in the mirror, and saw that her bearing was deceitful, her figure reedy, and that she had the hypocritical face of a tomboy.

FOURTEEN

MADO'S mother was a short fat woman, loving and obsessed with her family's stomachs, which she liked only when they were stuffed to the point of indigestion. Mado's father had a Machiavellian laugh and a tenor voice ravaged by senility. Her uncle was called Gustaphasse and was also her godfather. Mado's uncle's wife still had beautiful eyes. Mado's sister wore gold jewellery and showed off her breasts. Mado's brother worked in computers. Mado's sister's husband liked money and heavy Bordeaux wines. Mado's brother's wife was insignificant. Mado's nephews would wreck the tinsel on the Christmas tree. The Christmas tree was a spruce.

In the midst of these odours of family happiness and moose tourtière, Dominique felt cosy but out of place, like a penguin adopted by friendly Inuit. They had all sung "*Ca, bergers*" and "*Minuit, Chrétiens*," they had played Trivial Pursuit and, while the old people got their thrills at midnight mass, they had attacked and torn apart the wrappings of their gifts; now, enriched by a few useless possessions, they were wolfing down the food.

Mado was sitting right next to Dominique, her leg pressed against his, radiant in her white dress and brightened hair. From time to time she took his hand and squeezed it very hard, without regard to what he might be manipulating—that is how a heaping spoonful of cranberries got spilled on the beautiful damask tablecloth, unleashing a little girl's wild laugh in Mado and a little boy's grand confusion in him.

"It doesn't matter," Mado's mother, who was a saint, assured him. "It's all on its way to the laundry. Dominique, would you like a little more turkey, tourtière, some stuffing, shrimp aspic, a drop of wine?"

"No thank you," Dominique paled.

"Pass me his plate," Mado's mother said to Mado, "I know how timid he is."

"So," Mado's sister attacked, turning her aggressive chest towards him, "you're in the middle of writing a novel."

"Y—yes."

"Is it a romance or an adventure story?"

Mado giggled. "Come on, Dominique doesn't write simple things like THAT! What interests him are the complex convolutions of human souls and the relationships between the forces that regulate the intercommunications of male and female individuals!"

"You mean no one's going to be able to understand it?"

"I mean to say," Dominique meant to say.

"He means it's nothing like the candied drivel you usually read, my poor Louise, did you understand anything at all about his last book, there you had magnificent Gothic grotesques, UBUESQUE, the critics wrote, ubuesque, do you even know what that means and furthermore can you name me a single Quebec writer other than Jéhane Benoît, EH?"

"I don't see what that has to do with it, how excited you get, and besides you're getting ugly and fat, do you think you're starting menopause?... I just want to know what the Goddamn novel is about."

"ABOUT? But why in hell's name do you insist that it's ABOUT something?"

They kept arguing this way endlessly, aiming friendly perfidies at each other which might have been knockout blows except that the sisters were thick-skinned and used to it; at the beginning Dominique listened open-mouthed, because in some vague way he was the cause of it all, then he gave up. He searched for a conversation he could get more involved in—the old men were talking politics, doubtless about Bourassa ("An asshole who's selling us out to the English!" vociferated Gustaphasse), the younger men about computer programming (computers having dethroned tanks when it came to virile conversation), the nephews were absorbed in rebellious amusements ("If you touch my transformer I'll punch you in the face!"), and the rest of the women debated the usefulness of red onions in game tourtières. Choosing from such a rich selection wasn't going to be easy.

Finally Dominique got up to escape a third helping of yule log, on which subject Mado's mother had just given him a threatening look.

He found himself sitting on the vestibule floor dialling the telephone number of Maurice's hospital room.

"N...yes?" said Maurice, his acrimony muddled and dulled by sleep.

"You were asleep, I'm sorry...."

"Yes."

"I wanted to wish you a Merry Christmas."

"Are you making fun of me?" Maurice could have flared. "Why not a happy death and paradise in a few days, if it exists, EH?" But he said nothing, at least for a brief moment.

"Where are you?" he finally asked.

"At Mado's parents."

"You're having fun?"

"A bit."

"Good. I'm sleeping. Thank you for calling, my boy."

And he hung up.

Dominique ended up in the living room, across from the Christmas tree. There is nothing more insolent than a Christmas tree spreading its forest smell right in the middle of a living room, beside the television set. It's a low blow to the television; jabbering people and pasty faces seem ridiculous beside this silently shining magic. "My boy," Maurice had said. Dominique looked at the tree, completely absorbed in this internal music: "My boy, thank you, my boy...."

"Now you're laughing all by yourself?"

Mado draped herself over the arm of the chair, and the stink of her perfume frightened off the tree's smell. Condemned to be loved, Dominique suddenly thought, not without sorrow.

"I'm happy too. Your presents to me were...extravagant."

She wasn't alluding to the silver necklace, or the venerated and expensive Cohen he had given partly to himself in giving it to her. She was thinking of their amorous relationship, which had recently gone through a very carnal upsurge, Dominique having once more become a sexually operational being, thanks to you, Beelzebub, father of universal copulation—though thanks to Dr. Frolette, Mado naively thought. How could she have suspected that as they frolicked Marie-Pierre Deslaurier's bony face was being substituted for her own, that Dominique was making stormy love to an absent woman?

She was also thinking about that embryonic novel of which she knew nothing, except that its aura had begun to nibble away at Dominique, making him shut himself in his office every evening, his face full of pain. Of course she had tried to get a look at this work-in-gestation—"One of my secretaries could type you up a clean copy"—but she had run into a categorical refusal, and for good reason; he hadn't yet written a line. A trickster in every way.

It was this double trick that she most loved in him, he screwed and he wrote, therefore he WAS, and what's more, was hers.

"Do you remember?" she started, caressing his thigh, "do you remember our New Year's Eve at Sainte-Mathilde?"

"Yes."

"We stayed in for three days." She burst out laughing behind his hand. "Stuck together, inseparable.... The bed had become a battlefield.... And we battled so well," she added, her eyes half closed.

"Yes. *Avec le temps, avec le temps, va, tout s'en va.*"

"What are you saying?"

"Nothing. I was singing."

Everything had been put on plate-warmers or on the long pink marble table, and the observer could not but be impressed by the display. Comestibles, yes, but of such archangelic beauty that an aesthetic anorexic would have been turned on, a museum curator would have begged that they be preserved, stuffed on the spot for posterity. Truly a tempting feast. More than a little proud of themselves, Bob Mireau and Henri, the producer, white toque jammed over his skull, waved in response to the wild applause, congratulated each other with divas' smiles, swaggered about in front of their perishable masterpiece.

A gastronomic New Year's Eve. There were about ten of them—the entire "Not So Crazy" team and their legitimate or accidental other halves—and in Henri's dining room all their mouths were watering, their stomachs rumbling.

"Where do we start?" a technician asked, audaciously pointing his nose towards The Works.

"Back, you monstrous pig," scolded Bob Mireau. "First the introductions, you oesophageal boor."

"Yes," added Henri, "such costly extravagances must be presented, barbarians!"

"And not quite the way you have in mind, greedy holes."

"All right! Go ahead!" Henri said.

"No, it's your place," Bob said.

"All right. I'll start."

"No. I'll start. Because I did the starters."

Luc kissed Gaby's ears, so she missed the first words of the gastronomic presentation.

".... of three kinds of smoked fish: trout, salmon and sea bass, ladies and gentlemen, in their simplest dress, but topped with a crown of salmon eggs with sorrel.... Just beside those the special treat, the ineffable ragout of morels and goose pâté!"

"Recipe! Recipe!"

"Yes, the recipes," Priscilla insisted, taking a notepad and a pen in her white hands.

"It will take forever if you give the recipes for everything," Simone murmured timidly to her husband, Henri, who replied by giving her a dirty look.

"All right. Ragout of morels with goose pâté. *Primo*, you gather the morels the spring before from a secret grove in the Eastern Townships whose location I'm not going to reveal, ha-ha, do you take me for an idiot? *Secundo*, cook down the morels, dehydrate then rehydrate in sweet butter, stuff them with RAW goose pâté. *Tertio*, the sauce. You reduce water, white wine, cream, shallots, add a finger of port and cognac, reduce again. When thickened you add the stuffed morels until they begin to quiver. Season with care. Delicious. Applaud."

"Warm oysters with saffron," Henri cut in, longing for his share of the applause. "Count on six oysters per person, open them, put them on six rounds of aluminum foil after emptying them of their juice and cutting the muscle. Then the sauce. My God, the sauce....First, uhh, let's see, first ..."

"A tablespoon of chopped green onions, a glass of champagne," Simone whispered.

"SSSSHH! A tablespoon of chopped green onions, a glass of champagne, the juice from the oysters, put on a high heat and reduce by half. Cream lightly, raise into butter without boiling. Add a saffron pistil to the sauce. Put the oysters in the oven without cooking them so they are just barely heated. Dress each oyster in sauce. And that's it!"

"What does 'raise into butter without boiling' mean?" Priscilla inquired, "and where do you get saffron pastilles?"

"Tempura and other curiosities of Japan," Bob announced. "Ingredients: very large shrimp, calamari, fat onions, eggplant, sweet potatoes, green peppers, bamboo shoots, seaweed, two eggs, two small cups ice water, two small cups of flour. Mix the flour, honourable famished ones, with the eggs and the water, and you have paste.

Primo. Secundo. Mix the other ingredients into the paste, mix them well!... and brown them in the oil. *Tertio.* Dip the fritters in *ten tsuyu* sauce. Ah. How to make *ten tsuyu* sauce. A cup of broth, honourable idiots, a quarter cup of sake, two tablespoons of sugar, four tablespoons soy sauce and garnish with *yakumi*, which is, honourable imbeciles, shredded radish and ginger. *Arigato*!"

"Three-gourmet tournedos," Henri intoned. "For each person you have three filet mignons each a quarter of an inch thick: you grill them in butter until cooked to the desired point—I recommend very rare. Onto the first filet you layer foie gras with truffles, then the second filet, then a slice of sweetbreads cooked ten minutes in court bouillon, then the third filet, then raw beef marrow."

"A kind of Big Mac, then...."

"Silence!... Heat in the oven for ten minutes and cover with Madeira sauce. Madeira sauce: sauté onions and oyster mushrooms in a little butter, deglaze with Madeira, add consommé."

"And a little fresh tarragon," Simone added softly, "and some...," but Henri gave her such a look that she instantly stopped talking.

"Jewels of the sea *cardinale*. For four people. Triple as necessary. Knock out two two-pound lobsters and plunge them in court bouillon for five or six minutes."

"I could never do that to living lobsters," Patricia chirped.

"It's easier to knock out human beings," Gaby agreed.

"Take off their shells, cut them in two, sauté in butter, flambé in cognac. You add cream and fresh lobster bisque, cook until it boils. Fold two one-pound sole fillets in three, put them in with the claws, cook them in the sauce, take them out. Reduce the sauce and thicken with butter. Garnish the lobster serving-dish with the fillets of sole, the claws and the lobster pieces. Coat with the sauce passed through a fine strainer."

"Salade Henri-de-Nouvelle-France."

"Hey," Bob giggled, "have you just given it a new name, Narcissus?"

"Salade Henri-de-Nouvelle-France," Henri reiterated, unshaken. "Half a pineapple, two apples, 350 grams of Roquefort, 350 grams of salt pork, 350 grams of croutons, curly endive, radicchio, mayonnaise. Cut all the ingredients into cubes, cook the pork and the croutons in butter, put the lettuces in the bowl, add the cold ingredients, then the warm. Dress with diluted mayonnaise."

"He forgot the toasted almonds," Simone whispered furtively into Gaby's ear. "You always have to finish with toasted almonds."

"Queen of Sheba," Bob proclaimed, because people were getting restless. "Melt 200 grams of chocolate in a tablespoon of water, take off the heat and mix in 50 grams of butter. Meanwhile, beat four egg yolks with four soup-spoons of sugar, incorporating a large soupspoon of flour, whip four egg whites, add them slowly, then the chocolate, to the egg yolks. Cook in a buttered bread pan for twenty-five minutes at medium heat, use a needle to check that it's cooked through, ice with the help of two large coffeespoons of coffee, exactly, dissolved in warm water, add the melted ingredients, spread over the coffee, garnish with walnuts and almonds. That's all, you lowing plebes."

"There are also steamed baby vegetables, a parfait cov-ered in kahlúa, strawberry surprises, chocolate truffles, can-died chestnuts from Paris...."

"And for wine—everything! Just give a little listen to this, you idiots. A Château de Chantegrive '82 Graves, an Auxerrois Pinot, a Château la Commanderie Lalande Pomerol, an Aloxe-Corton '78, a Château d'Arlay Jura white, a Bruno Paillard pink champagne...."

They stuffed themselves for hours. All the marvellous dishes disappeared from the table and were delivered into dark and difficult metamorphoses. To aid their digestion, the company consumed quantities of hashish and cocaine, and traded subtle pleasantries just to stay in practice: "What's the difference between eating turkey and sleeping with Lise Bacon? Why do British pussies have Angora fur? One day a chlamydia met a gonorrhea..." Gaby was surprised to find herself laughing a few times; she was the only woman still convivially sitting around the table with these irresistibly brilliant men, except for Priscilla, who had her chair at an angle, her forehead furrowed with incomprehension. When she noticed this Gaby felt a jolt of pride—look now, little girls, see how well I fit in—then suddenly she was ashamed.

"All right, all right," she grumbled, "that's enough dirty jokes! Shall we dance?"

She wanted to take Luc with her, but he had evaporated to who knows where. She then resorted to Bob, who made a pretence of resisting, then followed her into a corner of the living room where they swayed politely to the music of Tom Waits. Since the time he'd told her about his problems, things seemed to have worked out with Priscilla; once more Gaby would catch them looking at each other, embracing hurriedly, whispering secretly between doorways—it was a strange relationship that seemed to prosper in darkness.

"So? Are you well?" she wanted to assure herself while they made a show of dancing.

"Extremely well. What a question!"

There was no question, especially since the night Bob had shown himself vulnerable, of further confidences between them; in fact there were no longer any questions between them, he would breeze through her office with an unbearable and distant affability and he would go to any lengths to appear happy.

She would have liked to admit to him, right there, that, to put it crudely, she missed their former camaraderie, the way they could laugh together, but as soon as he felt her eyes becoming serious and trying to make contact, he turned his head, then left her on the pretext that he suddenly needed a drink.

To hell with him.

Gaby danced a bit more, then stopped, overtaken by existential nausea. She wandered through the huge rooms until she found Luc in the kitchen, scrubbing pots along with Simone. Then she found Henry in the toilet, throwing up his guts. Priscilla and Bob she found in the boudoir, grabbing a quick feel. She didn't find Santa Claus anywhere; no doubt he had gone straight through.

It was crazy—the old lawn chairs stranded as though crippled, the stunned Christmas tree transplanted onto the balcony, the presents in the snow, the telescope posted like a sentinel in the corner, cold champagne and chips scattered plentifully about, and especially the two of them, wrapped in blankets that made them look like mummies—pleasant but completely crazy. Below them there were lights and people, no doubt warmly curled up; above them the Pleiades and Orion winked down sympathetically.

"How many stars do you see there, in the Pleiades?"

"Forty-three," Marie-Pierre said sarcastically.

In guise of a reprisal, Camille threw a chip at her head.

"Liar. How many do you see?"

"Seven."

"I see NINE!" Camille said triumphantly. "That means my sight is better than yours."

"No. That means you don't know how to count."

They played at who could make the other tip over in her chair, then who could drink her champagne with her head upside-down without spilling any, then who could recognize with her eyes closed the taste and PRECISE brand of the chips that the other stuck in her mouth. The champagne was courtesy of Gaby, the chips likewise; they'd just had to rummage through the cupboard where fifteen bags, all completely different, were silently hibernating.

"Hostess Mexican tomato!"

"No, it's Ruffles with bacon Hawaiian style."

"Shit."

Camille won at everything except drinking champagne upside-down, at which Marie-Pierre demonstrated a perfidious skill and a lot of experience. To congratulate themselves they declared that the ceremony of the gifts would now commence. From her father Camille received a camera, a nearly new marvel, very high quality and equipped with a telephoto lens; from her daughter Marie-Pierre received a coloured illustration she was not permitted to look at until she had looked into the eyepiece of the telescope.

"I'm giving you Orion M42," Camille whispered in her ear. "The sky's most beautiful nebula."

There it was at the end of the telescope, just as it was in the shiny illustration—a purple anemone lost in a splendour of blue-violet and black, a piece of magic torn from space.

"It's too much," Marie-Pierre said, impressed.

"I know."

To save heat they stretched out on the same chair.

"Merry Christmas," said Camille.

"Merry Christmas, my treasure."

"I feel good. But at the same time I feel bad."

"Ah?"

"Yes."

Camille burrowed her nose into Marie-Pierre's armpit as tiny shivers of anxiety ran through her.

"I wish I was like everyone else."

"What do you mean, like everyone else?"

"I don't know. The way other people are. Anemone Bouchard. Sylvie Tétreault. Everyone."

Marie-Pierre yanked at her hair to force her to turn towards her.

"You mustn't be like everyone else. You have to walk alone, in front, then try to find a road that no one else has ever taken."

"Why?"

"Because other people's roads never go far enough."

"Is that what you did, Papa?"

"That's what YOU have to do," Marie-Pierre said evasively.

Camille lay down again, rolled up against her father, puzzled or reassured, in any case assailed by the beginning of a blizzard which had just reminded her of the glacial order of things.

And while Orion drifted off, Marie-Pierre sang lullabies in her broken voice. Camille's vulnerable weight on her belly gave her dreams of maternity and she was happy; go to sleep my frightened angel, go to sleep my little star.

FIFTEEN

So what did he have that was extra, distinctive, so much more than the others?

He had everything.

First of all, his hair. His hair glimmered with the reflections of God knows what sparkling demon and it seemed to move all by itself, liquid and autonomous, never touched by the surrounding dust or dirt. And of course his eyes. Green, which says everything. With depths and twists in the iris, full of inexhaustible energy that could follow you anywhere. And his figure, his torso, his limbs, everything that is understood by the word "body": perfect, alas, perfect from tip to toe. And so seductively presented: today in a cloth and astrakhan coat, yesterday in a large cherry-red parachute vest, and in incredible sweaters with football-player shoulders, and pants you would have said were made of silk, at least five pairs of brightly coloured leather boots, daring clothes from expensive Western boutiques but worn so casually, with uncalculated indifference, an artistic I-could-care-less, as if they were old and worn out. TERRIBLY attractive.

Camille was concealed near the lockers, taking advantage of a rare opportunity to observe him at leisure. Some administrator, endowed with a sense of provocation, had put up mirrors throughout the school. In one that resisted the shattering energy of these beautiful young rebels, she saw Lucky Poitras. Sitting on the floor near his locker, in the company of two girls and an older boy— insignificant nothings able only to drink up everything he said and vibrate weakly to his beat. Lucky Poitras was talking, his voice full of honey and charisma, and while he talked he was swirling a deck of cards with the quick movements of a magician.

"Zaragoza, New York or maybe Florence," he was saying. "There's a school in Florence, they only make you do what you do best: if you're a good musician they turn you into a super-maestro; if you draw well, they help you become a second Picasso. No academic idiocies to drag down your natural talents!... If you don't know what you're good at, they find out for you. It seems that's the place where all the geniuses of the future go."

"Fuck!" said one of the girls, tremolos of ecstasy in her throat. "And that's where you would study?"

"Maybe. I haven't decided. I'd also like Paris, but my father says nothing's happening in Paris anymore...."

"It's true," babbled the other boy, in a last effort to gather a bit of the two girls' stupefied admiration. "It's all over for Paris, I read it in a magazine the other day...."

If only he would go away, go as quickly as possible, Camille kept saying to herself, let him be swallowed up by those amorphous cities, monster droseras that gobble up their victims and inject them with a poisonous perfume of nothingness and unreality, let his damned charisma evaporate for good in Beirut-the-bloody or Oriximina-the-Amazonian....Because she couldn't stand it anymore, the anxiety and the pain every time she saw him. I'll never love anyone again, Camille told herself, no one will ever be as beautiful as him.

"Not before next year, anyway," Lucky Poitras concluded.

"Ah, Europe," one of the girls exhaled.

"Europe, or South America ..."

"Or Asia. Asia is also supposed to be great."

"Jakarta, Istanbul ..."

"Wherever, but away from here."

"Yes, away, AWAY!"

They all shivered together, touched by nostalgia for what they would never know, places where life celebrated without them, adorned like an Arab courtesan, volcanic jungles and grandiose revolutions—how is it possible to be and become in the drab Montreal slush? From his pocket Lucky took out a small bag, a mirror, a razor blade.

"Straight from Lima," he smiled. "Ninety per cent pure."

The eyes of the others lit up; Camille's strained to understand what it was all about. Ah yes, now she saw: the white powder, extravagantly expensive. They were going to suck it up their nostrils, guaranteed happiness. Lucky began clicking happily on the mirror while the others held their breath. Lucky pushed the mirror towards the older of the girls.

"You start. You can do two lines."

He also gave her a bill rolled up like a straw that the other boy took care to smooth out.

"A hundred? A real hundred-dollar bill?"

Lucky, a bit bored by this amateurism, shrugged his shoulders.

"So? My father gives me one like that every two days."

"Damn, you're lucky," the other capitulated.

Nonetheless, this father seemed absolutely ordinary, he looked preoccupied and grizzled, dressed like a civil servant, inhabited a modest bungalow Camille had often looked over because the Poitrases lived just a mile away from her. Anaemic mother, no special glow. One child, unique in every way.

After sniffing his first line, Lucky held himself for a moment with his eyes half closed, then opened them and aimed them abruptly at the mirror, the big one, the one through which Camille was still playing Mata Hari.

"Do you want some, Star Wars?" he asked, his smile delicately mocking.

Camille immediately pushed herself back, catastrophe, he had been aware of her presence the whole time, the traitor, and he hadn't given it away, how could she ever forgive him? She ran off awkwardly down the other corridor, annihilated by humiliation and by that unbearable nuance in his voice, cutting irony, yes, but even worse, commiseration and pity, how could she ever forgive him?

Math test, the second of the winter term. The teacher handed out the questionnaires, moving sideways, a burlesque crab in a tie, to spot any suspect movements on the part of his victims, because he was old and had an inordinate hatred of cheating.

Sitting at the very back, Camille was considering set theory. In her way. That is, she was mounting a mental inventory of the things that distinguished her from the group made up of the other girls. The exercise promised to be futile. Let's see. The group had breasts. The group wore pants with a low crotch, and the padded shoulders prescribed by fashion. The group used makeup. The group liked "Dynasty" and sailboards. The group responded to the same incomprehensible jokes and shared the same passwords. The group idolized Prince and Ozzie Osborne. The group had friends, sexual partners and big plans for motherhood. The group had fathers who looked like men. The group always knew how far not to go in order to stay in the group.

Good. In all that, was there something repairable, did she have any reasonable hope of overcoming these various disparities? Hardly, to say the least. Her breasts refused to arrive and Ozzie Osborne's music gave her a headache.

While the ancient teacher, despite his suspicions and his lateral means of moving forward, moved quickly closer to her, Camille made a sudden and irrevocable decision: she was condemned to being very different? So be it. She would be so *totally*. Her position at the rear of the pack gave her no hope of being integrated? Very well. She would go to the front.

"Here," the old professor laughed, dropping the questionnaire on the table, "something to add to your collection of zeros."

Camille did not deign to reply, contempt wasn't worth the time, ancient crustacean Mathemethuselah.

"… mille … matics … cheat … amille …"

It was exciting, and it threatened to shake the comfortable foundations of modern astronomy: the universe might not be in constant expansion because of the original Big Bang, but the cause of the motion of the thousands of galaxies in space might be that they were being sucked into a mysterious force, an enormous mass circling within the confines of the cosmos. Not ejected from the past but energized towards a future collision. Not exhaled but sucked in. This enormous mass magnetizing us at a speed of six kilo-

metres a second—would it become the face of our apoca-
lypse, the great impenetrable and terrifying face of God?...

"... alk ... chologist ... mother...amille ..."

There were seven who were in favour of this revolution-
ary theory, and not stupid, either, no, seven reputable astro-
physicists renowned for their wisdom, at the universities of
Cambridge and Arizona, at the very professional
Dartmouth College, at the national observatories at Kitt
Peak, Lick and Greenwich.... Only one woman among
them: Sandra Faber from California. More and more
learned scientists were joining their number and their
cause, allowing themselves to be seduced by this concept of
a "vast convoy" hurtling through the sky, because a brilliant
hope had just been kindled, that the solution could be found
by looking ahead, not behind, that the rising generations
could join in the assault on the overwhelming TRUTH.

"... cheat ... amille ... CHEAT... peak!..."

She must write to this lone woman among the seven, the
homina faber at the Lick Observatory in California, she
would have to ask for more complete explanations, offer to
help and collaborate with her.... Because the obscurity,
come to think of it, was still almost total, the enigma had
been inverted, where did these innumerable celestial bodies
sprinting so madly towards the mysterious gravitational
force come from?

"CAMILLE! I'M TALKING TO YOU!"

Behold, the enemy had just lost his cool, the enemy was
giving ground. Camille turned an eye in his direction: J.
Boulet—because it was him, inevitably—was wearing a
smooth Buddha smile, but his bluish eyes were full of poison, no doubt he regretted that the strap and torture were
no longer available for educating children. She resigned

herself to returning to the mawkish sub-basement this man occupied, the story he had invented was starting to bore her, and threatened to keep her shut in here for centuries.

"I didn't cheat," she said, loud and clear.

"Ah? Well, let's see then," J. Boulet rejoiced. For him the slightest denial was orgasmic because he could hit back hard in return. "I only want to believe you, believe me, you know how much I'd like to trust you."

He stood up, revitalized, went to lean against the window, ended up against the plant that had succeeded the assassinated *ficus elastica*—a *philodendron pertusum* whose huge leaves, Camille noted, were unable to repress a repugnant tremor on contact with him.

"Explain one or two little things to me," J. Boulet said. "I don't understand so well. Since September, zero in everything, or almost. Then suddenly, in maths and physics, the same day, BINGO!... Knowledge blooms, marks better than perfect, a hundred per cent, ah ah sweet Jesus, how funny it is, how easy. So?"

"What?"

He was amazed she would speak. It upset the paedagogical method he had finally found to use on her. Trying to adapt himself to this new symptom, he mentally leafed once more through the encyclopaedias that had fed his career from the beginning, and doubtless explained why his skin was the colour of papier-mâché—Chapter XLVIII, book 3, subsection b): How to deal with schizophrenic children who used to refuse to talk but who talk now—wait a minute, my J., you'll be more upset when I'm finished, Camille thought contentedly.

"I want to know who slipped you the exam questions," he finally said, succinct and cold.

"No one."

"I don't believe you."

Camille cleared her throat with hypocritical deference, then also stood up.

"In group E," she began to recite in a monotone, "are defined operations which, with the help of two parts, permit a third to be obtained. If A and B are two parts of group E: 1) the intersection of A and B, called A inter B, is made up of the elements of group E that belong to both A and B, which is called the group of common elements; 2) the combination or recombination of A and B, called A combination B, is made up of the elements of group E that belong to A or to B, that is, to at least one of the two. As a result, if X belongs to A inter B, therefore X belongs to A and X belongs to B, and if A is included in B, A inter B = A. Moreover, A, B and C being three parts of group E, the difference between the elements of group E that don't belong to E is a part of group E called the supplementary part of A. It is written E-A: C A\E when there aren't—"

"That's enough," said J. Boulet.

"Electromagnetic waves include gamma rays according to their length—from 0.005 to 0.25 angstroms, X-rays—up to 0.001 microns, ultraviolet rays—from 0.02 to 0.04 microns, visible light—from 0.4 to 0.8 microns, infrared—from 0.8 to 300 microns, radioelectric waves—from a millimetre to several dozen kilometres; and all these waves travel, in the void, at a speed of 300,000 kilometres a second and oscillate according to a parameter of...."

"THAT'S ENOUGH, I SAID!"

He had more than paled, J. Boulet, his big white face with its patches of hair, illuminated by two demented pebbles, oh no, it was not a pretty sight.

"You'll have to get used to it," Camille said serenely. "From now on I'm getting a hundred in everything."

She turned her back on him and walked out of his lair. He did nothing to keep her back.

She hated them.

Sometimes it woke her up, she could feel it inside her, an undefined weight parasiting on her stomach like when you've had too much to eat. Pregnant with a two-headed hate. It sucked out her energy but fed her in return: when she looked inside herself she saw freakish osmoses which would have terrified more than one geneticist.

They often met, in what they stupidly believed to be perfect secrecy. Every Wednesday evening, at Michèle's house. When they thought Camille was far away with her father. But Camille had picked up the underhanded practice of coming home earlier, it was such a masochistic luxury to catch them unawares through the windows, to spy for hours on their gummy promiscuity. They would telephone each other, too. The childish giggling, the trailing little voice Michèle put on for these ugly occasions. Other times Michèle would go out to meet him, claiming there was a legal meeting or inventing some other stupid pretext. You just had to look at her to know, foolish happiness written all over her face when she stole away to meet him.

They traded a bit of mucus, felt each other awkwardly, like blind prudes. They talked a lot, at the same time, instructive conversations.

"Not normal," said J. Boulet. "Poor little Camille, so far from normal ..."

"Yes but, but brilliant marks now, first in the class in everything now ..."

"Exactly!... Duplicity!...Worse than anything, duplicity."

"It's true. Duplicity," Michèle sighed, wringing her hands.

"She lies to you. She has been lying to US for months, pretending she knows nothing.... Lies are so unhealthy."

"Exactly, speaking of lies,..." Michèle agreed weakly, "it seems to me, don't you think, what would you say, I would SO like her to know...for both of us...."

"Let's wait a little longer. I feel in her, how can I put it, there's still some distrust ... regarding me...." (Oh the wisdom of idiots!)

"It's because she doesn't know you....The poor child hasn't had the chance to really appreciate masculine contact, really masculine, you know..."(Oh the annoying stupidity!)

What could she do, where could she strike, how should she make the two-headed enemy crumble? Camille ran desperately from one window to the next, aiming the only weapon she possessed, the telephoto lens of her new camera. J. Boulet and Michèle groping each other on the sofa. *Click.* J. Boulet delicately taking hold of Michèle's right breast. *Click.* J. Boulet alone and meditatively picking his nose. *Click.* Close-up of J. Boulet's fat buttocks, naked and livid like in a horror film. *Click.* Close-up of J. Boulet's dick, a comma lost in the bush. *Click.*

When the opportune moment arrived, she would let them know. This edifying collection of photos, blown up and artistically framed, would look good on the walls of the school or, say, of the Board of Education, always eager to be more intimately acquainted with its employees.

It was a black stretch limousine, a kind of bird of prey poised on the snow.

"Deputy minister's limousine," Marie-Pierre laughed. She had an eye for tasteless things.

They were on their way back from the Odeon bistro, bellies well stuffed with illicit gastronomic delights—as they were every week—and the snow swirling down had drawn them to walk for a while on Mount Royal. Serenity and beauty. The city become metaphor, the dream of a dozing squirrel in a maple tree. And then suddenly, at the corner, they saw the car. A beautiful shining object in a no-parking zone, inside which two silhouettes appeared to be dancing.

"Let's go back," Camille said, fearing gangsters and terrorism.

Marie-Pierre gave her a harsh smile.

"No danger, my little chicken. They're much too busy."

"Why? What are they doing?"

There was a large and a small silhouette in the car; the larger was embracing the smaller almost violently. Marie-Pierre was about to lead Camille away, but then she shrugged—after all, the spectacle of life is for all to see.

"There are sharks," she said. "They buy bodies and they eat them."

Camille looked at her, terror in her eyes.

"I was speaking figuratively. It's not exactly like that."

The smaller silhouette had just emerged and closed the door, the limousine began to purr as it manoeuvred to leave.

"And the fresher the body," Marie-Pierre said with an additional touch of bitterness, "the happier the shark."

"Ah. You're talking about prostitution."

"Yes," said Marie-Pierre, amazed. "You're right. Things should be called by their names."

She took Camille's arm to invite her to continue their walk, but Camille stiffened, obstinately standing her ground. She was looking at something inconceivable: in front of them the gleaming limousine was spinning through the snow; left behind, walking with the heavy step of an adult oppressed by life, was Lucky Poitras.

SIXTEEN

THE words fell like dead weight: behind them, behind their little corpses stacked politely in the room, loomed feelings that would never see the light of day; the unsaid lurked and mourned, and that was what he had to listen for, with all his strength.

"Winter," Maurice said.

By that was understood: I'm cold it hurts come to my rescue Christ be damned anything to once more see Lafontaine Park, its buds exploding into flowers and its odours of lilac, I would give anything imbecile idiot what are you waiting for make me a miracle.

"I brought you some Belgian chocolates," Dominique sighed.

He meant: look how I'm doing my best, for the love of God let's talk about something else at least let's talk, let's try to establish some minimal link between us why haven't you ever been interested in my existence?

"Sadistic treatment," Maurice said. "Damned chemo makes you sick to your stomach like a drunk, me who had a full head of hair look at me, gang of murderers, ordered to leave me in peace, for once they listened to me, the imbeciles, have just realized they were making me sick by insisting on taking care of me, want to sue them for abuse of power and criminal weakening of the organism, what do you think?"

He meant: am I that sick?

"So take it easy," Dominique said, "trust others just a bit, try to sleep, I'm going to try to get you a private room, if you like."

He meant: yes.

Six months at the most, that had been the doctor's verdict. Maurice was infested with metastases, and that was the reason they had agreed to cut off his chemotherapy. Only the pulmonary complications were keeping him in the hospital; as soon as these symptomatic disturbances had been dealt with, he would be free to die wherever he wanted.

Dominique observed him without emotion. Emotion was not acceptable. Nor was fear. Maurice was still too much himself, alive and atrocious, to imagine that the day might come when he would be otherwise. Death was still an abstraction in which Dominique would be unable to believe until it had arrived for good, and then it would be too late, he could find no logical relationship between an inert rigidified carcass and a living breathing being, nothing credible linked these two distinct entities—apple and pear, horse and calf, vaguely related in form and that was all. And it was the same thing for a number of vague concepts—old age, notably, old age was an illusion and a mystery: how could he believe sincerely that Maurice had once been young, for example, that somewhere in a buried past Maurice's face was something other than this ravaged cesspit, UNTHINKABLE, totally unthinkable, people are either born old and sick or young and forever beautiful, UNABLE to metamorphose to this point, otherwise the whole thing was monstrous, life was monstrous and abominable.

Near them, a welcome diversion: Maurice's companion,

in misfortune and at the hospital, his bed at a right angle to Maurice's, was eating an apple. That is, that chunks of apple were sputtering and exploding from his mouth but it was unclear what was disintegrating so spectacularly, the mouth or the fruit.

"I'm going to kill him," Maurice said. "Tell him to stop or I'll kill him."

A force of nature, Dominique exulted; even in his death agony, even exhausted right down to his marrow, his father had the energy to hate. There he was, aiming his animosity in the direction of his roommate with all the conviction he could summon—struck by Maurice's cold fury, the unhappy man stopped masticating.

"Deaf and dumb," Maurice fulminated. "That man is DEAF AND DUMB! Ha! He makes a bigger racket than an army of dinosaurs on the march, than a tribe of hysterical monkeys, he doesn't eat, he splashes, he doesn't drink, he gushes, he pisses buckets and when he sleeps it's a million times worse, before I'm out of here I'll kill him, he's invented a new way of breathing—*buh-GARR, buh-GARR*—and his blood, would you believe it, the blood that flows through his veins makes a terrible gurgling noise you'd swear there was a snowmobile roaring through his veins…why are you laughing?"

"But, but all the same, Papa, you're not going to forbid him to exist…"

"LET HIM EXIST LESS LOUDLY! There, close the curtain, just seeing him is enough to pierce my eardrums."

Dominique obeyed, after looking carefully at the one-man band: he was quite young, with a joyful face that jarred with the anaemic surroundings. A woman had silently entered the room and stood next to him. Using sign language they were having what seemed to be a very cheerful conversation. Dominique watched them for a moment: their hands, fluttering in the air, had a serenity stronger than death.

Maurice was looking intensely through the window: the grey of the parking lot and the sky, dirty snowbanks turned on their sides like dough-rolls made of garbage, sickly light losing strength without ever having fully emerged.

"Winter," he began complaining again.

Dominique straightened up from the chair and put on his old anorak. Right now he needed to be free and outside, to be taking in the oxygen, however imperfect, of Rue Jeanne-Mance.

"I see her everywhere," Maurice suddenly said. "She comes in at all hours of the day, she hides behind the nurses, she talks in the doctor's voice, she looks at me through the curtains, I even see her at the bottom of my plates, in the mirror, in the toilet bowls..."

"Who are you talking about?"

"But the worst is at night." Maurice's voice was no more than a low anguished hiss. "At night she comes and sits right on my bed, I feel her, an icy weight cutting off my legs, oh God in his cursed heaven, every time she comes closer, when I close my eyes she appears on the other side of my eyelids, she's everywhere, black, horrible, the more I cry out in my dreams the closer she comes, I see her all the time I tell you, even right now for the love of Christ she's in front of me I SEE HER IN YOUR EYES!"

"Calm down," Dominique said, and held his hands as you do those of a child who is having a nightmare.

"Sshh ... don't say her name," begged Maurice, gripped

by terror, "whatever you do don't say her name, talk to me, say anything at all, I'm afraid, HELP ME!"

What words could he invent, what could he do? With all the world's powerlessness on his shoulders, Dominique began, his voice trembling, to recite the first verses he was able to remember, they were from Prévert's *Cortège*.

"A golden old man with a watch in mourning.... A snake in the hand with a bird in the grass...."

Maurice had closed his eyes, almost calm, just one small crazy vein was dancing on his temple, crying out for help.

"My skin is soft. Feel it. Feel it there where my neck and shoulder come together, there where it glows like a nectarine, where it's delicate. That's enough. I am soft like that all over, believe me, my softness is so amazing it will become legendary. It's inside that I have my teeth and my scars. Yes, inside, that must be something to see, barbed wire and stalactites, slashes all sewn up crossways. You can't have things like that done to you and get away with it, they're bound to leave their mark somewhere. At least things look as they should, my dear, aren't I satiny smooth, as smooth as someone who has never been touched?

"I was eighteen years old when my life was turned upside-down. From within. Mark that down. Eighteen years old. The great age. The useless age of the beginning of nothing, so far as I was concerned. At eighteen women explode from everywhere, the body is a celebration, love opens them, embalms them, oh how I hated them, how I hated their sensuality and that primal scream that made them reborn.... They were intercepted by life and they could plunge into it head first, you see, while I, I was an abandoned envelope, I was a dead woman—but with the same appetites, the same urges as them, perhaps even more woman than them, but condemned to oblivion because of this body, this miserable cursed body.

"So I fled inside myself, to the place where I was a woman and didn't need breasts to prove it. I pulled the curtains around myself. Gone the world of appearances, bodies, the lie of how things seem. The life of the mind, learning, research....I got such good marks at the Faculty of Sciences that they were flabbergasted. At McGill, Yale, Oxford, Cambridge, the Sorbonne: I got everything, at all of them—best student, scholarships, honours, the rewards of success....I became a dynamic thinker. The Brain of America.

"I sometimes long for them: my exciting little cells, my amoebas, my spiral treponemas, my beautiful trypanosomes. Like a game of Logo, metaphysical traffic: you look in a microscope and there they are though you never knew it, they are totally engaged in their little parallel trips and have nothing to do with you. Bacilli are so geometric you would think they were made of plastic. Foraminifers have extraordinarily beautiful rosettes. Radiolarians look like snowflakes. To recognize each other they sniff each other, like dogs, they shove each other around, they stick together, they link up in chains, spider webs, square dances, happily eat each other, oh they live a joyous life above all suspicion. And discreetly. That's what I like about them. Their discretion. Their simplicity. Don't laugh. Their authenticity, if you want to know: in life on our scale, no being can exist without calculations and machinations; but microbes exist for the sheer joy of it. Shit! We always need goals, desires, fabulous ambitions, we are so sickening. And arrogant. Me, for example. When I isolated the haematozoa responsible for leukemia, when I identified the first Alzheimer's virus, I rushed to shout it from the rooftops, to write treatises, give speeches, produce books. I was showered with honours. Splash! Which didn't prevent me from feeling like a criminal, afterwards, when I looked at my haematozoa and my virus in the microscope, when I watched them innocently going about their business, they who had trustingly allowed me to penetrate them so intimately; it was as though I had committed treason. Oh, it isn't easy to be pure. Had it been possible I would have wanted to become not a woman but an angel. An angel, my dear. Could an angel give you an erection?"

"If he looked like you, absolutely," said Dominique.

That was how things were with them. The point of no return, Dominique thought. Every week Marie-Pierre set him on fire. She was offering him her life on a verbal platter but alas, that wasn't enough, he would have made a pact with the most terrifying divinities and thrown his soul to the Devil—had he been persuaded that he had one—if She would just deign to go to bed with him once. She didn't want to. Of course, She was outrageously familiar with him, allowing him to touch her arms, her neck, to kiss the inside of her elbow or other inoffensive places, treating him like a domestic animal one feels affection for but keeps at a maddening distance—perhaps because of fleas. Or bacteria.

"The other day," said Marie-Pierre, "a man told me I looked like Saint Perpetuity—you know, Felicity and Perpetuity, the martyrs who were eaten by lions?"

"What man? Someone you slept with?"

"Of course."

"How many do you have like that a week?" Dominique ground out.

"As many as possible," She replied sweetly.

"Why not me?"

"You can't mix things. What I need from you is the way you look at me. And part of your heart."

She was pacing in front of him. Every time they saw each other there was a moment when She stopped talking and started wandering around like this, very slowly. She turned about herself, languid, catlike, exhibiting herself. She would also, sometimes but not always, get undressed. Purposely, in front of him, so that his view of her would be complete. "It's a game," She would say, "look at me as though I were a statue, an image." She would smile without a hint of perversity.

"Men don't know how to look," She said. "Right away they need to touch and grab."

"But what about me? I—"

"You? That's right, what about you? For you I'm a capital She, aren't I?"

"Yes."

"That's what pisses me off," She said gently. "I want to be a lower-case she, just a she and nothing more. I want to be grabbed, even if I detest it. I like a man to be big and hairy, with powerful shoulders, I'm filled with clichés and wildly attracted by machos. I want to be worshipped by gigantic brutes, delicately stroked by huge hulks. I want Sylvester Stallone to weep while kissing the hem of my dress, oh, just imagining Sylvester Stallone in the act of weeping and kissing the hem of my dress makes me wet. That's how I am. It's a curse."

"I see," Dominique sighed.

But he saw nothing, other than the fact that he would never be sufficiently virile for her; he had scarcely two hairs on his chest, and even they were blond, which destroyed any shadow of manhood.

"When I was a man," she continued, sitting down near him, "when I was a pretence of a man, I never looked at anything either. I didn't want to look at anything, as I've told you, my whole life consisted of putting slides under my microscope. Then one day I looked up: surprise! A woman was beside me, I was married to her and I hadn't even noticed!"

She burst out laughing as if at a hilarious trick, carrying Dominique along, making him forget for a moment that he had only two puny hairs and not a shadow of a chance of one day sharing her bed.

"What that proves," he said, "is that not paying attention can be a mistake."

"You said it. What's more, from that moment on I was taken over by fear, believe me, I instantly became part of the external world to be sure I'd never again be caught not looking!"

She became more serious and nestled her shoulder against Dominique's, oh the burning heat that emanated from her.

"Competitive people have something magnetic about them," She said. "Michèle, for example...."

"Personally," Dominique admitted humbly, "I'm the least competitive person I know."

"Michèle," Marie-Pierre continued, taking no account of his confession, "Michèle has always gotten what she wanted and has always wanted what she couldn't have. She had her first bicycle when she was two, her first car at fifteen. She studied international law in a Japanese university reserved exclusively for men. She became the principal partner of the biggest law firm in Montreal. And she got me, me, without doubt the most unattainable of all her objects. Oh, competitive people are so admirable, fate bends to their whims or they break it in two—*snap!*—like so much kindling.

"Michèle met me when my brain was starting to rake in fame by the shovelful, and she fell feverishly in love with both of them. My brain and my fame, bound together like Siamese twins. Nothing is sexier than notoriety, you should know that. At that time not a week went by without my name being mentioned in a newspaper or on television, microbiology was on its way to becoming more fashionable than Pink Floyd. It was embarrassing, everyone looking at me—you see how I've changed since I took on this new skin …in some way Michèle offered me protection from the others. In exchange, through me she participated in the great forward movement of modern science, what an incredibly fair bargain, don't you think, dearie? Aside from that, she was an agreeable human being, always dressed with unusual elegance, I could easily see us eating beef Wellington washed down with a Cabernet Sauvignon on a Saturday night, and on Sunday we might have a lively discussion about trichonomas and beneficial bacterial scum. Oh what a happy team! No? I thought so."

"But, but—with all that," Dominique stammered, "between you, the…what… that …"

"….bed? Yes, of course," Marie-Pierre sighed. "That could have been a problem but Michèle turned out to be very reasonable, very patient; you see, I had almost convinced her that I was purely cerebral, I sincerely thought so myself. Almost, I say. At the beginning the shadow of the Nobel was hovering over me, and what's a vague sperm transfer next to the shadow of the Nobel?

"But there was no Nobel. Shit. I say shit for her, because for me—well, it didn't give me so much as a wrinkle on my left buttock, don't frown like that. The evening she learned that it was an American who had gotten the Nobel, she wept every tear in her body, poor cow. 'How could they do it to us?' she sobbed. For the first time fate had thumbed its nose at her, she was deathly disappointed and in revenge she started to want other unattainable things—but ABSO-LUTELY unattainable ones—like demanding that I behave differently with her, that I be more manly, you understand, yes, more of a MAN, me! What a sinister joke life some-times is. And we started to be very unhappy together."

Marie-Pierre went and poured herself a large glass of cognac without offering any to Dominique, then swallowed it in a single gulp.

"I'm tired," She said.

"Wait," Dominique begged. "Do you mean you never slept together?"

"That's so important for you. All right, yes, my pretty, maybe once or twice. And the child came right away."

"You had a child?" Dominique went pale.

"Why not? What have you got against children? The survival of the species must be ensured."

With small greedy movements, her tongue licked the rim of her glass.

"It's not a child, anyway," She added, smiling, "it's someone very old and very wise, much more so than you or I. Why are you looking at me that way?"

"I love you," Dominique said, and Marie-Pierre distract-edly gave him a hand that he tried to crush between his own.

"You think you do," She said. "In reality, it's not me you love."

"What do you mean? I LOVE YOU!"

"You love the idea I represent, you love in me the woman with a capital W, that's what it is.... My dear, you are tremendously excited by my capital W. Don't count on me to solve your problems."

"What problems?" asked Dominique, alarmed. "What are you talking about?"

"Well, if you insist. There are all sorts of trouble spots in you—you can smell them. Think about that the next time you're holding your little lady against your heart, and your cute little thing is as flat as a harmless mollusc. And now, out, my pussy willow, I think I've seen enough of you for today, off you go, please."

Dominique went over to Saint-Denis and walked down it just for the sharp pleasure of being pushed about by the wind and wading through the slush at intersections. The salt attacked the old leather of his boots and the diarrhoeic snow was admirably suited to finishing the job. Shivering and soaked to the bone, perhaps he would be distracted from his more internal discomforts.

What was She trying to insinuate, why did She want to wound him when he was offering her his heart stripped bare? Ingrate. Traitor. B...bitch, that was it. Bitch, bitch. One day he would be able to hate her. She thought he was a homosexual and too cowardly to admit it, what a wild imagination, what Gallic extravagance....

Was he?

Half-suffocated by the cold, Dominique Larue began to look closely at the young men swiftly zigzagging along the sidewalk, tried to imagine their velvet thighs, their small firm butts, their.... dicks, okay, dicks, rods, penises, aroused, getting aroused, but nothing at all, not even the ghost of a flicker of the beginning of desire. Reassured, teeth chattering, he turned his lubricious fantasies towards the young women galloping down the street, bundled up in animal skins....Bum, crack, nipples, tits, vulva, splish-splash, pussy, pussy willow, meow meow!

Again nothing. He felt nothing.

So what was he? What kind of animal or vegetable? Could he ever be stirred by someone other than a transsexual? What, oh Lucifer, exactly what was he, and so long as he was asking the unaskable, WHO WAS HE?

A wino standing at the corner of Saint Catherine revealed to him that he was the grandson of Jacques Cartier and Lady Di. And it only cost him a dollar.

That night Dominique Larue started to write, this time for real.

SEVENTEEN

ICE door, she said to herself. Rosewood. Heavy and ornamented like a florentine, with cherubs in relief, bevelled panels, a knocker in the form of a dragon's tail. The door of an aristocrat. Or a social climber. Paid for by her, in fact, years ago, because she used to live here, behind these round-cheeked cherubs who rolled their salacious eyes in the rosewood. Marie-Pierre stepped back, the better to judge the totality of the architecture. Incredible. That she had lived in such an immense thing, capable of containing several growing families. Even worse, this thing had been hers, in the days when she was passing for a man. My house, she hissed sarcastically. Fixed in an idiotic perpetuity, condemned to the past. The windows had been repainted, that was all. Even the apple trees had hardly grown, judging by the few haggard branches that emerged from the snow.

It wasn't too late to turn around and go back. The house had suddenly taken on a terribly familiar look, the distant past was sniggering behind the windows and the ornate door; Danger! screamed the little animal that sleeps inside each of us, DANGER! DANGER! called out the muscles, the entrails, the vertebrae of Marie-Pierre. Hypnotized by anxiety, she began to retreat, prepared to take flight. At this exact moment the door opened and Michèle appeared.

Shock, undeniably mutual. They looked at each other, stunned. Michèle was wearing something mauve and silky, very pretty, that went with the bourgeois grey of the stone—she had always known how to melt into the decor, what a mineral aestheticism she had, in a former life she must have been a mosque or a Phoenician temple.

"Come in," she said impassively.

Neither a greeting nor a preliminary grimace. So be it. After all, they hadn't seen each other for eight years, though it might as well have been the night before, or a mere two thousand nine hundred and twenty-two days when you're in love.

"How are you?" Marie-Pierre smiled. "You seem to be flourishing."

"I didn't ask you to come here so we could discuss how we're feeling," Michèle said soberly. "Give me your coat. You can keep your boots on if you wipe them carefully."

She hadn't changed anything. Not the smells, not the vestibule, not anything else Marie-Pierre could see at first. Here, time had worn white gloves—perhaps it had even abstained from passing by. While she had fought unimaginable battles, torn between death and the agony of being born, everything in this house had continued to warn against the vanity of change.

Marie-Pierre put her purse on the pedestal table, the same table fitted into the same spot.

(Pierre-Henri Deslauriers put his attaché case on the pedestal table. A moment during which everything subsided into silence. In addition to his attaché case, he was abandoning the world of the infinitely small to penetrate the world of respectability. The vestibule exuded its smell of well-controlled panic.)

"Let's go into the living room," Michèle suggested.

Through all this she had been performing ocular miracles to avoid looking at Marie-Pierre. But once they were face to face in the brightly lit room, evasion was no longer possible; her eyes fluttered, began a frightened dance but finally came to rest on Marie-Pierre.

"My God," she exhaled weakly.

"It comes as a bit of a surprise at first," Marie-Pierre acknowledged gently. "But people soon get used to it."

She congratulated herself for having borrowed some decent clothes from Gaby that toned down the extremes of her femininity. Michèle looked her over a final time, her eyes now under control, then forced herself to look elsewhere.

"I'm not intending to get used to it," she articulated carefully. "Let's get to the point."

"Of course," Marie-Pierre said, pointlessly.

"I could have advised the police, I assure you it wasn't that I didn't want to, in any case I still can. I find it disgusting, you dirtying Camille with the mud you're wallowing in, it's much more than I can put up with. You've sunk low, Pierre-Henri Deslauriers, very low."

"MARIE-PIERRE. What's this about, would you do me the honour of being more explicit?"

"It's about a criminal act, it's about THEFT, receiving stolen goods, corruption of a minor, is that enough? Does that mean anything to you?"

Michèle wasn't shouting, you couldn't say she was shouting, the decibel level of her voice remained more than acceptable, but she was releasing violent sounds that pierced a lot deeper than the eardrums and Marie-Pierre found herself deafened. The miracle of hate.

"I don't see," Marie-Pierre said dreamily, "no, corruption of a minor, I don't really see—"

"Don't play with words, I'm talking about CAMILLE, and THEFT, I knew you'd try to deny it.... What do you call someone who stuffs his face at a restaurant and then takes off without paying? Well, Pierre-Henri Deslauriers, would you at least have the courage to answer me?"

(Answer, Pierre-Henri Deslauriers. Dig down into that dark web you have where a brain should be and pull out some answers, dead or alive. Why don't you love me, why don't you ever take me the way women are supposed to be taken, where is your life going and with whom, what terrible secret lies behind your silence?

And that younger Michèle was waiting in torment, might have been waiting that way for centuries because Pierre-Henri Deslauriers had nothing to give, especially not answers. Now the gods of matrimony had transformed this house into a tribune of the Inquisition, now all the rooms, the vases, the molecules of the house were relentlessly chanting *why why why why*....)

"We were walking quietly along the street when this man appeared from nowhere and grabbed Camille, braying out that he recognized her, and then yelled *Thief! Thief!* IN THE MIDDLE OF THE STREET at rush hour, you can imagine how edifying that must have been, how much I must have wanted to disappear into the ground, the owner of the Odeon was knocking my daughter about as though she were a criminal, I had to calm him down, pay him back on the spot, three hundred and twenty-five dollars, oh I was so humiliated, I'll never be able to forgive you the humiliation I felt, THREE HUNDRED AND TWENTY-FIVE DOLLARS!..."

"I'll pay you back," said Marie-Pierre in a low voice.

"Oh? Really," Michèle laughed. "But that's going too far. You're being too nice."

Unpractised in sarcasm, her face almost immediately resumed the required expression: one of dignity overcome and deep pain.

"And the camera?" she sighed. "The camera you stole and dared to give Camille, which is now at the police station because I had my suspicions and, unfortunately, how justified they were! It's been reclaimed by someone, I had to pretend I found it in an alley, they were good enough to believe me"—especially since there's not so many alleys in this district, Marie-Pierre couldn't help thinking—"how low you've sunk, Pierre, how miserable...."

What could she reply, how can one argue with the righteousness and cruel logic of people who have everything, bank accounts and shining consciences? One can't, of course, several revolutions have already made futile attempts in that direction.

"I didn't steal the camera," Marie-Pierre said humbly. "I swear it. Someone gave it to me."

This was the amazing truth. Three nights before Christmas, while Marie-Pierre was killing time in a bar, a man with bulging eyes had sat down next to her, casually looked her up and down for an hour while knocking back a dozen beers, then suddenly entrusted her with the bag he was carrying. "I'll be back in ten minutes, Fatal Treasure," he had murmured. "Keep this for me...." Two hours later he had still not returned and Fatal Treasure had kept the bag—which contained, incidentally, the camera and two or three related objects.

Michèle found this explanation so pitiful she didn't even bother to contest it.

"You understand that in the circumstances," she concluded professionally, "there's no longer any question of your seeing Camille, even from a distance, or speaking to her or trying to approach her in any way. Until she reaches her majority. My lawyers are taking this seriously; any attempt on your part will be considered criminal harassment and punishable by imprisonment."

She busied herself taking inventory of her nails—ten, she had ten of them.

"We have nothing else to say to each other, I think. Consider yourself lucky…lucky to get out of this so easily."

(Zigzagging and drooling through the enormous universe, a persistent little crawler who fell a thousand times and each time got back up, Baby Camille was heading towards her final destination of the moment, Pierre-Henri Deslauriers, who stood dizzyingly erect in the living room. "Ma-ma!" she lisped, arching amorously on her knees, "MA-MA-MA…." "You have to say Papa," Michèle corrected from far away, "PA-PA-PA…." "MA-MA …," baby Camille called out stubbornly, hooking on to the crease in his trousers, and Pierre-Henri Deslauriers, touched by grace, took the little crawler into his arms and waltzed her through the huge intergalactic cosmos of the room.)

"They're pretty, your curtains….Lace is always so airy…."

Any sentence would do, for the moment; it was a question of sealing off her emotions, carefully pushing away reality so it would lose its edge, give her some time. What had been said? Had someone said something, why was this house filled with the nauseating smells of phenol and sweat? Where was Camille? Camille. That was the name of the nasty pain clawing at his stomach: Camille. Marie-Pierre gained control of herself again.

"Good," she said, and she tried a few steps on the soft carpet. "That will be,"—she weighed her words, careful to be precise— "that will be very painful....For her too, you know."

A strange noise, nearby. Marie-Pierre looked around; it was coming from Michèle, a kind of moaning seemed to be churning in her throat, arguing with itself about whether to come out.

"Are you all right?" Marie-Pierre asked worriedly.

The moaning increased, was on the point of giving birth to frightening things, sobs or maybe howling, but it suddenly stopped entirely, reined in by an iron will.

"No, I'm not all right," Michèle breathed, "not at all, you've always made sure I felt guilty, I feel guilty about everything with you, as if everything were my fault, but just the same what happened is not my fault, everything that has happened to you is not my fault, are you going to say that to me one day, will you ever tell me that IT'S NOT MY FAULT?"

"But of course it isn't your fault, calm down, dear—"

"DON'T CALL ME DEAR!" screamed Michèle, and then she really did begin to weep, the floodgates open wide.

(Michèle's tears surged up from some deep place, as though from another time. "Don't cry, dear," Pierre-Henri tried to appease her. "I don't want you to become a woman," Michèle pleaded, "I can't have been so mistaken, why does this have to happen to me?"

Pierre-Henri Deslauriers put his hand on the inconsolable back of her neck. "It's happening to ME," he would have liked to point out, but the inanity of these words was too obvious, people are condemned to travel side by side, their parallel sorrows under their arms.)

"She hates me," Michèle sniffled, trying to at least appear more in control, "she's always hated me."

"No, don't say that...."

"I turn myself inside out for her, I would give her anything, I GIVE her anything, but it's totally useless, it's too unfair, children are so unfair...."

"She's going through a difficult phase, pre-pubescence, you know that," Marie-Pierre recited awkwardly, astonished to hear herself.

"NO! I don't know," Michèle spat out, claws sharp. "Why doesn't she hate you, tell me that? You've never taken care of her, NEVER, why aren't you the one she hates?"

Michèle considered her silently, as though for the first time, and some of her defences fell away. "I shouldn't hold things against you," she murmured. "You've always been good and gentle and honest with me, it's true. I know that with my mind. If I were good too, I wouldn't be angry. But I'm not good. I'm torn by the past and by Camille and by the feeling that something in my life has gotten away and I can't recover it. Now go. I don't want to see you again.... Marie-Pierre."

But let's keep on trying for a bit anyway, a bridge might be constructed between our two respective ditches, let's get together for real, as though this carnivalesque marriage had never happened....But the words were blocked before they could be spoken, GO AWAY repeated the Chippendale armchair the grandfather clock and the eternal table, GET OUT MARIE-PIERRE chorused the curtains carpets and tiles, the furniture, the decorations and even the shadow of Pierre-Henri Deslauriers, which was standing stiffly at the top of the stairs.

So she left. A voice whispered, "Good luck," while she

closed the door behind her; she turned around but no one was there, just the rosewood cherubs giving her a sympathetic wink.

EIGHTEEN

INCE love had erupted into her life, Gaby had been doing well. She had lost six pounds, at night she slept like a baby, her eyes looked clear and rested. Most of all, her anxiety had disappeared, that sluggish anxiety that eats away at the lonely, doubtless to punish them for not being able to endure the company of others.

Love was keeping her busy. Now Gaby no longer envisaged weekends as no man's lands paved with uncertainties, nor did she allow herself to be dragged down by the television news, which was always showing some half-starved or charred face, some nonconsenting victim of the planet's inevitable hazards. Who would have guessed such happiness could come from simple things: to know who you were going to eat with and sleep with on a Saturday night, to know nothing about any boors with the bad taste to be suffering somewhere at the same time.

In his wake Luc Desautels brought order, calm and cleanliness. Also many other things, to be fair, but the first three virtues deserve to be underlined because they are so rare in men, let's admit it, even if it is sexist.

Weekends were generally at his place, with times for excess and times for continence, the whole range, in brief, in a rhythm which allowed everything its place. For example, if one night they splurged on foie gras and red meat and fish with mayonnaise, the next day they nibbled at raw greens. If there had been a lot of drinking on Friday night, Saturday was devoted to water. When they found themselves awake and in full flight at three in the morning, they had gone to bed at ten the night before. So splendid was the universally applicable rule of alternation that not having known it sooner was an unpardonable sin. One weekend in two was consecrated to outdoor activities, the other was given over to the smoky pleasures of the city. An evening of repertory cinema was inevitably followed by an evening at a mainstream film, Pierre Richard following Tarkovski, because, in Luc's faultless logic, you should never miss anything because you never knew at which door the masterpiece would appear.

Gaby had found it very easy to accommodate herself to this new and happy order; henceforth she knew where she was going, enough of blind wanderings and killing indecision, and besides, her liver was also feeling better. Of course a small part of her, buried deep, totally ignoble, couldn't stop itself—before movies for example—sadly staring at buttered popcorn and finding it a lot more attractive than raw carrots, but heroically she resisted and health always triumphed over vice.

When it came to sexual roles and domestic activities, the wonders never ceased. The new man had finally been born and Luc Desautels was a tantalizing prototype. Not only did he espouse Gaby's most intimate claims, but he found them inadequate and went further—feminization of terms was absolutely necessary, ALL the overly phallic aspects of the French language should be reconstructed, the priestesshood and the women's papacy should be established without delay, God called She, women given the best places during battle, Ms. General, birth control pills and tampons covered by health insurance of course and—indisputable necessity—daycares, BILLIONS of daycares spread through the cities and the villages, the mountains and the valleys. Gaby listened to him open-mouthed, pinched herself inside to make sure she was alive, looked between the legs of this incredible Luc to be sure the unequivocal swelling was in its place. So little imperialism in a man can never be taken for granted.

The bristly division of duties posed no problem, never would: he did everything. Gaby's participation was limited to peeling a few vegetables and occasionally cleaning the counter afterwards, while he ran all over the city shopping for groceries and bargains, tamed the dust and dirt, rendered order out of chaos, put soups on to simmer, tied the roasts, twisted the pasta, seasoned the sauces, set the table, insisted on washing the dishes with one hand and drying with the other, recleaned the counter after Gaby, EVERY-THING, as we said, and that was no euphemism. At the beginning, gripped by female atavism and cultural guilt, Gaby tried to intervene. One time, while he was lingering in another room, she made a sneak attack on the dishes; it wasn't long before he discovered her.

"Leave that," he said.

"Of course not," she laughed.

Amorously, first one, then the other, they insisted, arguing over the privilege of getting the grease off the bottom of the pots—it was becoming ridiculous, and Luc seemed to bend. Without entirely breaking, because he lurked in the corner of the kitchen, observing. After a moment Gaby, who couldn't stop looking at him, saw that he was unhappy.

"What's wrong?"

"Hmm?" he smiled. "It's...nothing."

Lilliputian silence.

"There," he finally said, sadly pointing out the glasses. "There are spots. And the utensils, sweetie. You should. If it's possible. If they don't get dried right away it leaves rings, look, it's terrible, they're dirty all over. I can take care of it if you want, sweetie."

Sweetie wanted, this time and all those that followed.

Mondays, Tuesdays and Thursdays were off-days because of Gaby's work, which often continued into the night, but without fail they telephoned to exchange a few loving words. And Wednesdays Luc slept at Gaby's, to provide a libidinous break in the interminable week; maybe it was the metaphysical influence of the surroundings, the colour of the walls or the enticement of rising feminine perfumes, but on Wednesday evenings, for whatever reason, they made love a lot.

Luc brought the same disciplined care to sex that he applied to everything else. He liked passion to be judiciously enclosed, otherwise, how could one distinguish humans from raccoons? I ask you. For this reason lovemaking always took place in the bed, and always in the same one or two positions, those that had proven themselves. A few times Gaby ventured to try some subtle variations, but he resisted, as recalcitrant before her fantasies as a cat before water or a Hindu facing a Tamil.

"Wait a moment, for God's sake," she nonetheless tried to slow him down one Wednesday, as desire prepared to lead them towards the bedroom. "Can't we do it here against the wall, or half dressed, just for a change, or on the kitchen table or on the floor, shit! WHY NOT ON THE FLOOR!?"

Luc considered her for a moment in silence, chagrined by the sharpness in her voice.

"If you want," he said.

Obediently he stretched out on the floor. Gaby followed him. But nothing good came of it, without the spice of spontaneity nothing was left but the hardness of the bare wood, and, aching all over, they got up to carry on in bed.

That was how Luc Desautels was. Charming, lean, much less perverse than average. Certainly Gaby had known more inventive lovers. But no one, ever, had looked at her that way while making love to her, in fact no one before had ever been *making love*—and to tell the truth, that was worth a lot of perversions.

"It's a total disaster," Marie-Pierre was saying, her eyes happily fastened on her *entrecôte béarnaise*. "Women struggle for their independence but in our hearts, my dear, we all dream of being supported—"

"No!" Gaby objected. "What are you saying?"

"Haven't you noticed?" Marie-Pierre's voice began to purr. "Next time you're in a restaurant, watch when the time comes to pay the bill....It's wild the way women start looking away, poor little darlings, they seem so unconcerned. Even in Lise Payette's television serials, the Liberated Women never take out their wallets to pay for the cocktails."

"I can guarantee you that Luc and I pay for everything fifty-fifty."

"And that makes you happy?"

"Of course," Gaby lied.

It was midnight, this Thursday evening, and they were sitting at the table in the company of a few amicable bottles of wine and some very brotherly half-cooked meat—eating with Marie-Pierre meant a cowardly retreat from broccoli and its green merits, but Gaby didn't complain too much.

"The Chinese understood it, psychological drives are contradictions, yin and yang, those concepts are useful. Take you, for example. Pass me a bit more of that sinful crusty bread, my dear. Thank you."

"What, me?" Gaby stopped chewing.

"And the Boursault, pass me the Boursault, it's so perfectly runny. Aren't you having any Boursault?"

"Yes. Take me, for example. What does that mean?"

"It means you have a very very strong yang side. But of course there's nothing wrong with that."

Marie-Pierre contemplated Gaby and her piece of Boursault with smiling tenderness; then, satisfied, she burped.

"And what does that mean, a 'very very strong yang side'?" Gaby broke in hesitantly.

"My God. It's part of how you are, that's all. Yang is movement, external, warm, functional, active, it's the male principle of the universe, as you probably know."

Gaby uncorked another bottle of wine to celebrate the occasion. What surprises life holds; now it was revealed that there was a phallic power inside her, just begging to come out—no doubt she would soon start getting hairy.

"Are you telling me I'm a man but don't know it?" she giggled. "Do you think I should have an operation too?"

Marie-Pierre raised her eyes to the ceiling and held out her glass.

"Right away the melodramatics.... There's no doubt you're persnickety about it, you biologicals.... Everything is always black and white for you, it's so much easier that way.

The women on one side, the men on the other, swing-your-partner, do-si-so."

She sponged her own and Gaby's plates with the help of a huge crust of bread, added to it a morsel of cheese—about half a pound, for the texture— and two or three glassfuls of wine for the humidity, and it all disappeared immediately, *gulp!* between her hard-working jaws.

"It's a fact," she said, swallowing soberly. "There's a lot of yang in you. Multiple male drives wriggling around and you won't let them express themselves. That's bad."

Gaby gave her a sour smile.

"You're annoying me with your hair-splitting, do you know that? You're really annoying me."

"Yes," Marie-Pierre persisted, as though for herself, "fascination with power, the desire for conquest and death, it's very clear, what a shame to hold all that back, you're slowing down your whole driving force."

"Listen, I find your gobbledygook exasperating even if I don't understand it, and since you're talking with your mouth full it's making me sick. I'm putting on some music, okay?"

"As you wish, my dear."

Sleepy jazz began to penetrate the room. For a few seconds Marie-Pierre pretended to contemplate the music, but she was not going to be so easily silenced.

"Maybe it's a sign of the times," she took up sarcastically. "You're all the same. Male and female twined together inside but you deny that, you always struggle to stay faithful to your façade. It must be very tiring."

"And you?" Gaby said. "Speaking of façade. The man within yourself, what have you done with him?"

"For me it's not the same thing," Marie-Pierre laughed.

"He wasn't inside me, my male, he lived on the outside and I took care of him."

Suddenly she stood up, moved by the quarrelsome trombone that had just joined the piano; the music was yang and she wanted to dance. Gaby watched her with an expression she would have liked to be vindictive; there was nothing to be done, this hormoned thing, as Bob Mireau would have said, always managed to disarm her. Now, for example, her movements were jerky and arrhythmic—it should have been graceless but it wasn't. What she did and how she did it hardly mattered, the least of her gestures had an unexpected glow. Marie-Pierre seemed in TOTAL HARMONY with herself—that was it! An exasperating harmony that nothing could disturb. "That's why I went on your crazy-persons' program," she had confided some time before. "So the fact I'm so perfectly at peace with myself would disgust people. To sow doubts in the minds of the certain."

Doubts—she sowed them by the shovelful. Gaby was watching her dance and she was telling herself that it was inexplicable, she was becoming attached to this inexplicable being, this inexplicable being was becoming almost necessary to her.

Then she said, point-blank, "I would really like to meet your daughter."

Marie-Pierre stopped dancing. Came slowly back to the table and took the time to empty the bottle of wine.

"Camille?... She's on a trip right now. Camille is going to school outside the country, didn't I tell you?"

She lost herself in contemplation of the earring she had abandoned on the table at the beginning of the meal—made of chromium-plated metal, aggressively cheap, in the shape of a deformed bird—attached it to her lobe and looked for the other earring.

"Shit," she grumbled. "Do you see it anywhere?"

They searched in the empty plates and coagulated remains, crawled on all fours under the table, looked in the cracks of the floor, the fibres of the carpet. Nothing.

"Well, we'll find it another day," Gaby assured her, her heart in her mouth and the chromed bird enclosed in her hand.

She should have suspected something. In the entranceway, Mrs. Wagner had unfolded her batrachian eyelids in her direction; for two whole seconds, this morning she had chosen Gaby, kept her at the centre of her serpent's gaze. The event was rare and worrisome. And later, in the CDKP corridors, there had been Henri's bizarrely executed sidestep when he suddenly angled off towards an adjoining office rather than meet her. So it is that fate always slips us hints of what is to come, but we pay no attention; heads down, we go about our business, which was what Gaby did.

That day's business was a likable little old man who had been an assassin for twenty years, the way others do housework or make raisin pies. He had killed twelve people, just like that, for the Canadian government, he would say over the air, a beautiful profession, clean and discreet compared to being, for example, a torturer, and it left no bad smell; while waiting for capital punishment to be brought back he had retrained himself as a writer of mystery novels. Next there was this young woman, a specialist in long-distance hypnosis, whom Gaby proposed to keep for the end of the program, in case she really did succeed in putting the listeners to sleep.

Once these new examples of human insanity had been sent into the studio, the day was hardly begun; many others remained—some better and some more horrifying—to be flushed out and slotted into future schedules. It was thus in her guise as speedy and dishevelled galley slave that Bob Mireau surprised her late that afternoon, and he ventured into her office with the precaution normally reserved for cathedrals.

"Do you have a minute?" he asked respectfully.

Bob's presence had become so rare these last few weeks that Gaby, amazed, dropped everything—leaving her telephone receivers and her crazy people dangling.

"But of course. Hundreds, billions of minutes if you want them."

He gave her a thin smile and looked for a suitable place, among the newspapers spread out on the table, to sit down. But that didn't seem to make things easier. On the contrary. He sat with his backside cushioned on Wednesday's press and with horizontal waves running across his forehead, so silent it seemed he would never speak again.

"Beautiful day," Gaby tried helpfully. "Spring is in the air, don't you think? Yes?... Would you like to go for a drink somewhere, or get something to eat after the taping? Yes? No?"

"Don't have the time," Bob grumbled. "Maybe another time."

Then he jumped right in the water—splash—which at first made a few small waves.

"The BBM surveys say we're losing ground, did you read?..."

"Just a bit," Gaby said, unconcerned. "We're still in first place."

"It's unfortunate, just the same. That's the way it starts, a hundred listeners tune you out, then it's thousands, then it's all over, no, I tell you, it's unfortunate."

"It's not the first time, come on, Bob, we've always recovered quickly."

He was silent again, sulking; a lock of hair fell over his eye and he didn't bother to brush it away—a little boy, thought Gaby, a little boy who is funny and miserable and always needs to be encouraged.

"You're doing too much." She patted his hand. "You always do too much, you're the best host in the city, what am I saying, in the country, people would do anything to hear your velvet voice."

He pulled his hand back with a precipitousness that he tried in vain to camouflage.

"Exactly," he murmured. "This program is special, in fact it depends on the research, almost uniquely on the research, I know you work very hard, Gaby, I know how stressful that can be for you."

This time, Gaby understood. Huge waves were rolling towards her.

"Shoot," she said coldly. "Stop beating about the bush and shoot."

"Please understand"—he avoided looking at her—"I am very very very happy with what you've done until now, but research is an exhausting job, it demands constant innovation, sometimes a program like ours needs new blood, you know, to keep working—radio, you know, it's ruthless."

"Rotten, you mean. I'm fired. Do you have someone in mind to take my place?"

"Well," he blushed, "perhaps, but I haven't really thought about it, maybe, yes."

"Let me guess," Gaby chuckled. "I bet her name starts with P... P as in PROSTITUTE, as in PRISCILLA. Well?"

"Don't be vulgar," he sighed.

Then she cracked. She had an overwhelming desire to bury her head in her arms, to let go entirely, to be left limp and empty.

"My God, Bob," she said shakily, "I can't believe it. We've been a team for years, for years."

Those were the only words she could find, and she kept repeating them, *for years, for years,* and in fact they expressed all her bitterness and despair, the years of complicity, of looks exchanged and understood, hilarious laughter and the absolute certainty that you really were touching someone, underneath the mask—in the end, years of bull.

Afterwards she felt Bob Mireau coming close to her, touching her neck lightly, imperceptibly. His voice came to her as though from the next room, truly defeated.

"It's her. She wants your job, at any price. And I want her, at any price. Have pity on me, Gaby, have pity on me, I'm being dragged into hell."

NINETEEN

THE traps grew more numerous.

First there was spring. It decided to explode right at the beginning of March, the villain, and that disturbed many a precarious concentration, including that of Dominique Larue. Outside, it made everything smell of rebirth; even worse, it came indoors and the light, intense and robust, now lasted late into the afternoon. All this had its inevitable effect on the dark work of the mind. Even though he kept his blinds hermetically sealed and locked himself into the most shadowed corners, Dominique was overtaken by a biological spring that chased through his veins and whispered to him that he should be romping about instead of schizophrenically scratching at paper.

But the schizophrenic paper-scratching had born fruit, now was not the time to stop: two hundred and ninety-one pages were piled up in front of him, a monument to fertility still lacking too many pieces to be called a novel.

So, pulled by the missing pieces, pursued by the siren call of spring, Dominique Larue, despite his two hundred and ninety-one pages, was not happy. This manuscript was full of Marie-Pierre Deslauriers, it exuded her perfume, her crimson aura. To know how it ended, he needed her. But for the last while Marie-Pierre had been making herself scarce, coming back to sleep at Gaby's at unreasonable hours, no longer showing any desire to answer Dominique's questions or have him pirate her soul.

In these circumstances there was only one thing to do, as with teals: lay siege to it in its hideaway, where at least you can soak yourself in its smell, for lack of more concrete sources of inspiration. The researcher was obviously big-hearted, or else she was just tired of always finding him on her doorstep, carrying on his patient and useless vigil; she gave him keys to the apartment, so he could wait in comfort.

Every day since, Dominique had brought his manuscript to the Rue de l'Esplanade. Mournfully he watched the trees budding in Jeanne Mance Park, he chewed his cheeks, he reread his manuscript until he knew it by heart, he furiously explored Marie-Pierre's drawers in the hope of unearthing the missing fragments of his novel.

Marie-Pierre had few clothes, but lots of cosmetics and flimsy underwear in which her identity seemed to have taken refuge.

Dominique foraged through her silk panties and bras but he was not bombarded by lubricious thoughts. The trophies that rustled between his fingers marked, better than anything, the extent of the battle She had fought, the fragility of her victory. Furtively touching them he suddenly found himself in spiritual symbiosis with her, as though finally grasping some small bit of her reality, and he heard her voice again, the harsh inflections of her voice, so expert at calmly relating the most incredible stories.

"Just imagine," She would burst out laughing. "Imagine people's faces when I started to show myself as I really am! Horror and disgust! Help! Freak! The panic in the eyes of the little receptionist at the research centre the morning I came in wearing mascara and earrings! The metaphysical terror of all my worthy subordinates! Polite, oh everyone was so polite, with the good-morning-directors here, how-are-you-directors there, and jovial smiles that stammered; no, no, I don't notice anything unusual, but as soon as my back was turned it was chatter it was cackle it was panic, what my God is it possible, could he be going crazy?..."

She would laugh, Marie-Pierre, burying in her beautiful rasping laugh the humiliations and meanness of that bloody past, but Dominique Larue couldn't laugh, her cynicism gave him goose bumps.

"I thought I could get them used to it a bit at a time," She chuckled. "I told myself that with a bit of makeup one day, a little jewellery the next, a little skirt after a while, why not, they could get used to my new image a bit at a time, they would see that I was still the same brilliant-efficient-organized director, they would gradually accept my new identity and would love me more for it, and amid the general high regard and tender affection, sniff sniff, the chrysalis would finally become a butterfly. Bullshit."

Thus it was in presuming the existence of human tolerance and Santa Claus that Marie-Pierre had lost everything—her teaching position at the university, control of the laboratories, her job as Director of the Canadian Centre for Contemporary Research, the respect of her peers and, it goes without saying, all related privilege. The rout became so frenzied that it was hilarious, but some things still bothered her, like that letter from the centre's administrative council asking her to give back two medals she had recently been awarded, a letter to which She replied amiably that it was impossible, dear sirs, the medals were in use at this moment as nipple ornaments in her strip show. No doubt they had believed her, and they must have been delighted with her response since it was the kind of abject behaviour they expected from her.

"But I understand them, really," She added forgivingly, "because the truth is, my dear, I wasn't all that pretty during my transition period, half male half female and no way of knowing which was going to win out, my face raw from scraping and hair-removal, my Adam's apple sticking out above my flaming new breasts, the Hulk in the course of mutating towards a still faraway grace, I understand them perfectly, at that time I hated even looking at myself in the mirror."

That was when Dominique Larue had spoken about courage, he thought he remembered, about her courage in getting through those terrible times, and for the first time She had shown a flash of temper.

"What courage?" she had raged. "What for the love of God are you talking about? From the very moment I saw a transsexual on American television who claimed THAT was possible, I asked no questions, I jumped in as though into the fountain of youth, it wasn't a question of courage, shit, it was a question of survival. You mix everything up, you want heroism at any price, do you want me to tell you what would have been courageous? Keeping my male exterior to the end of my days, that's what could have been called courageous, that wonderful courage you admire so much!"

"You found her?" Gaby sarcastically greeted him.

"Oh. What time is it?"

"Two-thirty. In the morning, of course."

"Of course," Dominique sighed.

Once again he'd been caught by the researcher, his hands in Marie-Pierre's silky underthings; he no longer took offence, neither did she, each was careful to respect the freedom and the psychotic whims of the other.

"I suppose I should get home," Dominique suggested.

"Yes, your wife might be worried."

"We're not married," he said, as though to justify himself.

She offered him a coffee which he, as always, traded for a glass of water with lemon, and they sat down beside each other in the kitchen, which still stank of Marie-Pierre's carnivorous habits.

"I wonder what he's like," Dominique said.

"Who?"

"The man She spends her nights with—the MEN, I should say," he finished, politely sorrowful.

Every time they met by chance they spoke only of Marie-Pierre, particularly at the dying hour of the night, which seemed to belong to her alone. Dominique and Gaby knew very little about each other, which suited them perfectly; they had what they shared and it was restful not to look for more.

"There are no men," Gaby said tranquilly.

"Why do you say that?"

"Because I KNOW. She has never slept with anyone and she's not close to doing it."

"..."

"Virgin is what they call it," she said ironically, as though she were clarifying the matter.

"But," Dominique said, staggered, "her lovers, She talks so often about her lovers."

"Yes, and about her marvellous mother, Aster, who drowned. And her unknown father, who died when she was born."

He waited for the rest. The researcher expressed herself

with the friendly confidence of someone who isn't trying to convince but is simply telling things as they are.

"Her mother really was called Aster, and it's true that she died when Marie-Pierre was twelve years old. Drowned, that's going a bit far. Drowned in alcohol, shall we say: cirrhosis of the liver and softening of the brain. Profession: prostitute. A pretty enough woman, yes, if you like the fishwife type. Her father is still alive, in an institution. Seventy years old, fallen apart, completely senile. In his wilder days he was convicted of petty theft and tons of assaults. Irresponsible and violent—in short, the classic bad father."

"How do you know all this?"

"It's my profession," said Gaby. "At least it was."

Dominique didn't respond to the sudden morosity in her voice; it went beyond their common zone.

"And the rest, the brilliant student years, the Brain of America, the almost-Nobel-Prize?"

"Absolutely true. She fabricates here and there, you know, but it doesn't mean she's always lying."

"But then, how can we know what's true and what isn't?" Dominique worried.

"What does it matter? Are you writing a novel or a documentary?"

"I like the truth," he smiled weakly.

The truth—he wanted to laugh. The truth was that Mado thought he was at the library—some stay open all night, he had solemnly told her. The truth was that he compulsively avoided the house and the telephone—he had a panicky fear of the telephone, which tears the silence when it rings late at night to announce terrifying things, a father's death, for example.

And that was as far as they got this time. They sat curled

into themselves. Then Gaby opened the window wide; instantly the night flowed around them, the air laden with smells of the earth, urging them to silence.

Here the night was never total: there were lights that glared more harshly than in full daylight, there was the slamming of doors, incessant voices, noises of bodies battling to survive at any cost.

Maurice was terrifying to see. His skin was already the colour of a cadaver, his bones were asserting their importance by coming to the surface—but despite everything, in his eyes there was a spark of life that had no desire to abdicate.

"Sit down, don't be afraid, dying isn't contagious."

The telephone had eventually found Dominique. At night, or rather in the morning, at twenty to four, in the middle of a shapeless animal sleep, suddenly Maurice's voice: "Come. I know what time it is. I have things to say to you." He hung up almost immediately. "Is he dead?" whispered Mado, dishevelled, instantly ready for catastrophes and moral support.

Not yet, but death was approaching him at full speed—never had his father's death dared to show itself to Dominique so immodestly, so unbearably, amplified by pallid surroundings that didn't even try to camouflage the evidence. A room for sufferers that someone else, after Maurice, would impregnate with his own odours of terminal pain, and then the next, and the next.

"I don't want you to come back after tonight, I want to pass to the other side all alone, as I've lived, it's the only possible way for me, can you accept that?"

"Yes," Dominique said.

There were few happy images but some, nonetheless,

that scarcity rendered unforgettable—like that time Maurice had given him a fledgling bird, for nothing, for the pleasure of giving him something, and the time he had taken him to the circus, small fleeting lights in the fog of childhood, a smile, a gentle word, a hand on his shoulder, awkward and parsimonious gestures but gestures just the same, fond memories from the past to reinforce the vital bonds of blood, and to break the heart, Papa, my poor papa.

"Don't make a face, it'll be better for you after, there's nothing worse than dragging along a father who's not up to it."

His voice was so low that Dominique might not have heard had his attention not been painfully fastened to him, ready to seize the words even before they were formed.

"No," he tried to protest, but Maurice waved a tired hand to silence him.

"There's no more time to waste, this is not the moment to tell each other lies. I didn't love you and I didn't love your mother, there's only one person I ever loved, really loved, if you just knew, loved so much it still hurts, I have to tell you about it."

Maurice's eyes struggled tearily for an eternity while Dominique tried to calm the harsh convulsions of his breathing.

"His name was Julien, he was a man, a very young man, he worked at the bookstore beside our house and when I met him it was frightening and explosive. I've kept it all inside for so long that it must have gone rotten, you know, your father is a shameful old fag, WAS, because I'm not anything anymore, now I'm nothing. It lasted six months, six months of extraordinary ecstasy, I can't tell you how wonderful, six months of hiding from your mother and hid-

ing from myself….I couldn't go on, I saw it as an ugly for-
bidden thing but it was so bright and joyous, I couldn't confront that, or touch or love anyone else after….He cried
when I left him, I can still see him, Julien, he cried like a little boy but I've been crying the whole time since, thirty
years I've been crying in secret, Julien, that's what's so terrible, what filled me with poison…."

And Maurice began to cry, loudly and without restraint,
for once. Dominique kept sitting there, vigilantly watching
him, watching his withered hands make those small harmonious movements that inexplicably reminded him of Marie-
Pierre. Then Maurice grew peaceful.

"I'm going to sleep for a bit," he murmured. "You do me
good, I know you'll forgive me for not giving you more
space in my life. Go to bed now, try a little to be happy."

He seemed to be sleeping already when Dominique
kissed him on the forehead and left the hospital room. But
Dominique himself had no desire for sleep. He drifted for
hours towards the dawn, shivering and softly singing himself nursery rhymes.

It was two days later that the telephone rang again, and by
the way he had of clearing his throat when he felt overwhelmed by events, Dominique recognized the voice of his
father's doctor.

"Monsieur Larue?"

"Is he dead?" Dominique asked.

Silence and more throat-clearing.

"Not…not exactly," the doctor hesitated. "No, it seems
to be the opposite. He's well, he's even very well, his metastases have completely disappeared, like that, evaporated, we
just can't understand it…"

TWENTY

SHE wore bluuuue vel-vet
Bluer than ever were her eyes....

Isabella Rossellini's voice was not exactly what might have been expected to rise up from this soft and podgy body waddling on the stage, but the clients of the Nefertiti, none too picky about their realism, did not hold back on the applause. So much so that no one minded when the elephant stopped lip-synching for a moment to acknowledge it, leaving the voice of Isabella Rossellini to pursue, all alone, its threnody on textile loves. Except perhaps for Marie-Pierre, relegated to the back of the bar, who was always upset by amateurism.

She no longer remembered what she'd been looking for here; but one thing seemed sure: she wouldn't find it.

The place was similar to others in the south-west area of the city where she sometimes wandered. Neither less shabby nor worse. Its only distinguishing feature was that it accommodated transsexuals of all kinds, real and fake, finished or in transition. Mostly women—or at least presenting themselves as such—but exaggerated women, costumed and made up as though for a carnival, theatrical fauna who seemed to have come straight out of an old Michel Tremblay play.

The quantity of breasts was impressive. Everyone had them, round ones and chubby ones, some ample, some like mountains, everyone looked at everyone else's, inspecting them for volume and shape, speculating on the superiority of their own, hating those who appeared invincible. The hormones and silicones carried themselves high and firm. The rest of the anatomies, however, drifted in total ambiguity; hair showing through makeup, muscles emerging from décolletages, sharp bones reddening skin, and no doubt a number of zizis imprisoned under the skirts. The total effect was spectacular, a monstrous farce—so many monsters abandoned along the way by their Frankensteins.

A stripper had now mounted the tiny stage. PAMELA LOVELACE! the emcee—he/she androgynously garbed in tie and jacket—had announced. Wavelets of excitement passed through the audience; this Pamela Lovelace seemed to be held in high regard by her colleagues. It was easy to see that people here had known each other for a long time, regulars in this milieu of indeterminate sexuality; the clients whispered and called to each other across the room, over the head of Marie-Pierre, who stayed silently in her chair, her heart heavy with a pain she couldn't define. Then she understood: the problem was that she had come here looking for the comfort of belonging to some community, for a warm welcome that would at least momentarily break her isolation, but nothing had happened. There was just the painful feeling of being even more alienated, more excluded here, among her artificial sisters, than in the biologically normal world.

"Pamela isn't so bad," someone commented to her neighbour, both of them sitting near Marie-Pierre. "Too bad about her hair, have you noticed the way she pushes it up on her forehead?"

"Umm....Anyway, she has beautiful legs, a bit wrecked by her varicose veins but you can hardly see them...from a distance."

"I've heard that they had to redo her womb, the surgeon botched the job."

"So...she's going to have to stop stripping for a bit."

"Yeah. She'll lose her job here, anyway."

"Huh. No loss to us...."

They exchanged a sharp little laugh and Marie-Pierre wondered what stage of feminization they were at, under the gleaming furs moulded to their thighs, and if meanness of mind was yin or yang. At the same time, the two women she was watching gave Marie-Pierre a nasty look that made her retreat behind her fourth gin and soda. Above all, don't draw attention to yourself.

The problem with liquids, even alcoholic ones, is that they inevitably lead to the bathroom. For a while Marie-Pierre had been twisting in her seat, uneasy at the idea of crossing the bar between the rows of vindictive eyes—she who in any other place would have coquettishly tried to attract attention. But here, her intuition insisted, ostentatious showing off could be dangerous. Already her status as an outsider had made several people look at her closely; she was better off melting, like a chameleon, into the darkness. So she made use of the climax of Pamela Lovelace's number—the migratory waltz of the tiny undies over the deliriously enthusiastic crowd—to slide surreptitiously towards the bathroom.

Oh.

Camouflage might be possible in the dark and smoky bar, but here, under the cruel neon lights, among the multitude, the moment of truth arrived. At least six women were redoing their makeup, waiting for a seat to come available, smoking and snorting dope, shooting up—a syringe fell almost at Marie-Pierre's feet—chattering and laughing. And looking at her.

Oh those hallucinatory faces, those caricatures of women with their mascara too dark, their earrings too jangly, their mammary appendages too developed....

Freaks.

Marie-Pierre frantically searched for something reassuring to cling to, her own reflection in the mirror, perhaps, but she couldn't recognize herself in this jumble of faces, she saw that she was horribly like the others, horribly excessive like them, my sisters, my detestable sisters.

Her panic was so flagrant that some of the others began laughing, then all eyes converged on her.

"Where did she come from?" asked a tall black woman with a spiky mane.

She advanced towards Marie-Pierre, who retreated, numb, as though in a nightmare.

"Do you have a dick?" she laughed. "Or a slit? Eh? I'm talking to you. Do you still have your dick you cute little baby?"

She was purposely squeezing every bit of possible vulgarity from her words; the others were doubled over laughing.

"Show it to auntie," Spiky Mane repeated as she came close enough to touch Marie-Pierre, who had turned pale as a ghost. "I bet you still have it, your disgusting little dick...."

"No," babbled Marie-Pierre, "I—leave me alone, I'M NOT LIKE YOU!" she screamed as she fled the bathroom, and the Nefertiti, in such a rush that she left behind her purse, one of her high heels and many of her illusions.

•

The night was made for walking, walking without respite, but there would be someone at the end of the darkness, in stories someone always appears and then the romance begins. In other people's stories. But hers seemed so singular, totally askew, as though made by a blind carpenter, maybe her story was already sagging and couldn't support any new characters. That was a painful thought, like all the others that came to her as she randomly walked the lethargic streets. A few bars were still open, but she had been to so many these last few months that alcohol was coming out her ears—Oh the pressing need always to have other people looking at her, the need to believe in the romantic stranger who would never appear.

Marie-Pierre noticed that her traitorous legs had led her to the Rue de l'Esplanade, without her noticing. No doubt the researcher and the author were waiting there to spy on her—quickly she slanted off towards the park and the friendly shelter of the maple trees.

It had taken her long enough to realize.

It had started as a feeling, one of those transitory feelings that you chase away like sandflies because they don't seem based on anything, but that come back and stick. Stubborn.

The feeling of being watched. Even locked into the bathroom, even barricaded behind the door of her bedroom, even totally alone in the researcher's large apartment. The constant feeling of eyes on her, on everything she did, on her private parts. She had become extremely modest, no longer permitting herself any exhibitionism in front of the author or the researcher. But still, despite her new discretion, the uncomfortable feeling of being scrutinized through a magnifying glass.

Next were the people. Those she encountered on the landings, the sidewalks, near the local stores, even in certain bars; for the last while, seeing her arrive, they would immediately stop their conversation and remain quiet until she had passed; behind her back, these discussions, these whispers she could no longer doubt, this mysterious code to which they all seemed to have the key. And that concerned her; it was a strong feeling that was rapidly becoming a certainty.

There seemed to be some kind of link between these two feelings that couldn't get around. She had never been one of those weak-minded creatures who frighten themselves, she knew the weight of the rational and the tangible. But the incontestable truth had to be accepted: something was brewing, a complex whole of which she was seeing bits and pieces.

It was only later that she discovered the cameras.

Located in strategic places throughout the apartment, small black eyes suspended at the heights of her thighs and chest, near the toilet seats, in the shower, above her bed, in the mirrors, anywhere she was likely to undress or be naked. Everywhere.

And now she began to remember this or that suspicious thing the researcher and the author had done, taking turns to conceal the miniature cameras, secretly verifying that they were still in place, surreptitiously adjusting their positions when necessary.... Yes, it all added up, no doubt these cameras fed into a television channel to which people had access—that was why they stared at her when she walked close to them, that was what the malicious whisperings were about, they were laughing at the memory of the program of the night before, where, unknown to herself, she had been seen innocent and naked, stretched out on her bed or soaping herself in her bath....

Oh, she never ceased to be amazed by human duplicity, she who had thought she knew its every variation.

Marie-Pierre came to an abrupt halt. Once more the intense sensation of being spied upon. They had followed her here, even in the relative calm of the outdoors, they were closing in on her vital space. Nor was she surprised when she saw them standing guard near the tennis court, surrounded by projectors and a herd of indifferent technicians, already preparing to focus the cameras on her, wearing frayed and traitorous smiles, the author, the researcher, and even the child, a screaming disappointment, the child, who was affectionately gripping the fingers of Pierre-Henri Deslauriers, all united by their desire to make use of her....

She ran to escape the aggressive lights they launched at her, dancing wildly across flowerbeds, scraping her elbows on rosebushes, losing shreds of her dress behind her. She ran and then she stopped, her mind clear.

There were no pursuers, no cameras. The lights were on all sides of her because she was at the intersection of Park Avenue and Mount Royal, in the midst of a cluster of street lamps. She collapsed on the sidewalk, struck down by the terrible truth: she, the Brain of America, was going insane.

TWENTY-ONE

SHELTON. It was an unimpressive name, Shelton, evoked nothing special, made you think of a brand of cereal, fibrous and insipid. Nonetheless this Shelton, nasty cracked-wheat cereal, had just given his name to a supernova. That bastard Shelton, thought Camille. Englishmen are always the ones: he happened to be there, this Shelton, stupidly studying the sky, no doubt he had big teeth and pimples, and then it happened! He discovered a supernova, his name would go down in posterity and be inscribed in the cosmos for hundreds of thousands of years.

Life was full of injustices. Camille had promised herself to be the next in her century to discover a supernova; this seemed to her a reasonable challenge given the enormous number of hours she spent at the end of a telescope, making sure no suspect fluctuation of light passed unseen. Supernovas did not often keep company with humans, they weren't like strawberries, let's face it, they couldn't be harvested just like that, from a chance look. The last time someone had seen a supernova had been in 1604, when Galileo was alive. And now, since Shelton-Wheats had grabbed this one, what earthly possibility remained of getting her claws on one of these marvels?

A dangerous marvel, nevertheless, for those who came

too close. Think about it. If a star like Sirius, eight light-years away (a light-year being, as we know, a mere 9 trillion 460 billion 610 million kilometres), took it upon itself to become a supernova, to die, that is, it would mean unprecedented cataclysms for earth. A devastating nuclear explosion—but how magical!—that would suddenly transform this inoffensive star into a star ten times brighter and more fiery than the sun, burning vegetation and hair to a crisp, wiping out the ozone, drying the Atlantic, and putting an end to the crazy arms race.... (You wanted a bomb? Here's one, and it's natural, the ecologists can rest easy.)

What a racket, what huge sonorous upheavals must be propagated in an oxygenated atmosphere when a big star explodes. Camille tried to imagine the thing: the word "noise" would lose all meaning, and any human ear zealous enough to be present at the event would lose its faculty of hearing forever.

The night was clear. Castor and Pollux slid towards the east, Procyon was projecting its questioning light into space, Leoy prancing lightly innocent as a lion on a baby's cradle. Infinite and calming, this floating beauty would always be there, a source of strength, and Camille suddenly felt extraordinarily happy—despair was only a hollow term invented by people who never looked at the stars. She even had a friendly thought for Shelton-All Bran, on the other side of the globe, who was said to be unable to sleep since his first brush with mystery.

Nonetheless, these past few weeks despair had been showing its big ugly face, and it hadn't always been possible to turn it away. Oh, that first Wednesday of emptiness, trying to act as though nothing was wrong while he didn't call, and then it was six o'clock and Michèle, suspicious anxiety at the corners of her eyes, proposed filet mignon fries Brussels sprouts in butter her favourite dessert crème caramel and then it was nine o'clock and ten and midnight, Thursday Saturday Sunday and her father's silence became terrifying, a crime, a fatal accident. He would never be back, he was dead somewhere without anyone to close his eyes, and much as Camille tried to evade the enemy, she was quickly wasting away. To such a point that the enemy found itself mobilized, I beg you, Michèle in fact begged her, and then, seeming to know something, he's well I'm sure of it, I hear he has been very busy, I beg you to eat a little.

Busy.

That possibility was a thousand times worse than death, how could she eat and be alive if her father didn't love her anymore, not enough to at least throw her a few crumbs to show he was alive, how could she start hating him?... Then there had been the letter.

Not really a letter, some words scrawled on the back of a postcard and delivered in an unlikely way. One morning while she was on her way to school, the driver of the eight o'clock bus accosted her at the vehicle door. "Is your name Camille? A woman gave me this for you, stupid job, now I'm supposed to be a mailman, luckily she was good-looking."

The photograph on the card was of a night sky, the words said: "Be patient, my treasure. Am in the grip of circumstances beyond control. I'll be coming for you soon, when you are a woman. Marie-*Père*."

That was all. Sombre and implacable and informing her that the absence would be long and that its duration could not be appealed. But at the same time there was this guaranteed light at the end of the tunnel, her father loved her and would take her with him in a hardly conceivable future, so she would have to start living again to make the time pass more quickly. And Camille, as patient as a planet in the process of being born, went back to eating, sleeping, getting perfect grades. The enemy was relieved.

At this time, while Cancer displayed itself in the midst of the sky, this woman, her mother, occupied the house with her new partner. They now saw each other openly, no longer embarrassed to agglutinate in public. Now this man often ate with this woman, and Camille was obliged to be present at the abominable event. This had been arrived at by a series of sneaky manoeuvres, the way a grass snake slides into a bird's nest. One memorable springtime Saturday, Michèle, shining with emotion, had delivered the goods.

"I am very fond of you," she had begun, as a preface. "You are my unique and irreplaceable child, but a woman has needs, a woman, I am still a woman, a woman a woman, a woman also needs ..."

She was unable to finish, twisted up in blushes and maidenly sweat, and Camille, her face as closed as a knife, did nothing to help her.

"To fornicate," she finally said. "Say it, Mother, to fornicate."

Michèle then lost all her colour and the few words vegetating in her throat; she threw herself into tearful protests. "I love him," she said preposterously, "I love him and he loves me and I beg of you to let us live a little, I have suffered so from loneliness, and you already know him."

Yes I do, that transparent pear, that miserable overripe fruit, I know him better than you ever will. And when Michèle pronounced the loathed name of J. Boulet, Camille wondered how to react: to pretend she was shocked, let out wails of terror, threaten to stop going to school, flee the house—or to stay there like a worm, to perfidiously invade the beautiful apple of their romance? This last option did not displease her, and it was the only one with real possibilities.

"Let's try," Michèle implored, "let's try once or twice, I promise he'll amaze you, please, my sweet."

The once or twice had proliferated, she'd stopped counting to avoid vomiting, but the amazement still had not shown up. Disgusted, Camille had invented a constructive approach. Each of their communal feasts was now a terrain for experimentation, which she used with the subtlety of a savant searching out the chink in the armour, the Achilles' heel, of the Minotaur. This evening, for example, she had discovered that J. Boulet detested the squeak made by a fork carelessly drawn across an eyetooth or a plate. Way to go. The fork was henceforth devoted to miniature gymnastics which had undoubtedly eaten away at its outer coating, poor silverware. But very carefully and only from time to time, so that the operation retained its apparent innocence. J. Boulet suffered in silence, while sizzling the instrument of the crime with suitably heated looks.

"Astronomy is a wonderful passion," he managed with enormous effort, "very wonderful and good for you, you must spend hours like that, gazing at the shining stars without even realizing how much time has gone by, *flown* by... isn't that so, Camille?"

Squeeeaaak, opined the fork.

"Hours, you can say that—whole nights," Michèle jovially chimed in, "she would camp outside until dawn when it was 35 below if I let her, isn't that so, sweetie?"

Squeeea....

The efficacity was doubled if the action of the fork was

supplemented by a mouth left open to display food in an advanced state of liquefaction, or smackings of the lips, or some delicate and ceaseless sniffling giving definite signs that murky humours were clashing in her respiratory passages.

"NATURE OFFERS EXTRAORDINARY GRATIFICATIONS," J. Boulet boomed, to mask the ambient noise. "It's like me—gathering wild mushrooms, I can wander for miles in the forest to flush out *cantharellus cibarius* and *tricholoma flavovirens* and *rozite caperata* and *agaricus campester*, which are much better than *agaricus silvicola*—"

"But isn't it a bit dangerous?" Michèle worried. "Aren't some of them poisonous or even fatal?"

"Of course you have to know what you're doing; *amanita virosa*, for example, is distinguished by its satiny white colour and its volva and its unstriated edge and its odour of slightly faded rose, which allows you to tell it from *agaricus* HOLY MACARONI WHY DO YOU HAVE TO SCRATCH THAT WAY WITH YOUR FORK?!!"

"Wh—what, what's wrong?" Michèle desperately gulped out.

"I don't know, Mother." Camille shivered, her eyes plaintively angelic, in the touching voice of a young lamb being torn apart by satyrs.

The payoff came afterwards, in the form of a somewhat sharp exchange between Michèle and her gentleman lover in the bathroom, where they had manoeuvred themselves in order to be discreet. In vain, because Camille's hearing would have pierced padded walls in order to lose nothing of this melting climax that redeemed the drab meal a hundredfold.

"She's making fun of me," J. Boulet hissed softly,

"you're not seeing anything, I'm a man of great patience but she has a way of getting—"

"You're exaggerating, I know my daughter well enough to know when she's innocent and when she isn't, please, drop these mulish school-principal fantasies."

"Oh really, mulish school-principal fantasies," J. Boulet, beside himself, ground out loud and clear, "would you like me to leave right now, is that what you want, do you want the principal and his maniac manic-depressive mulish fantasies to get out of your life forever?"

Alas, the symphony had been but brief; an effeminate silence followed this virile exchange, and they made things up in each other's arms, I didn't I'm sorry I don't let me. But the day might come when the bitterness of the arguments reached a point of no return, when reconciliation became difficult, that was the goal to which she had to direct all her creative energies. She would search out the odours to which this man's unconscious was allergic and anoint herself in them from head to foot, she would sew lethal bacteria into the hems of his underwear, she would season the soups of this grotesque mycologist with buckets of *amanita virosa*— that poisonous name had not fallen on deaf ears.

While she waited, Cancer was there, above her head, prepared to offer her provisional escapes, and Camille turned the telescope towards it. The enemy had shown itself relieved to see her flee outside, perhaps she would be allowed to stay out late. And now—look! there, in the Crèche cluster—hadn't she just seen something flickering, maybe an embryonic supernova...

"Hi. Is that a Bok globule you're looking at?"

Lucky Poitras. Catlike, he had emerged from the darkness. Now he was standing a few feet away from her, his hands in his pockets.

"N–no," stammered Camille. "It's a…a…I was looking at the Crèche, a star cluster in the middle of Cancer, up there, you can see it a bit with the naked eye but not much because of the pollution."

Talking made her feel good, kept her feelings at a distance, so quick, find more words to make the miracle last and keep the apparition from vanishing.

"Peasants used to call it The Hive, and they used it as an infallible test of the atmosphere. Away from the city you can see about ten stars with binoculars. But with my telescope I see almost a hundred. Do you want to look?"

"Yes," he said.

He came close. Strangely, his honeysuckle fragrance was now just a trace, suffocated in coarse odours she didn't recognize. And now, close to him, she saw that his beautiful leather jacket was stained and torn.

"Where do I look?" he asked, his voice quavering.

That was when Camille saw that he was crying. Without a sound, as though in spite of himself, overcome by a deep pain.

She took him in her arms. He was much taller than her but was amazingly light against her small shoulder, she could have cradled him like that for hours, in her astonishment at being allowed on this other side of the armour, the place where men are fragile and tender and let themselves be consoled.

TWENTY-TWO

"THERE it is," the researcher affirmed.

She was pointing at the lower half of a duplex that had undergone a meticulously rustic renovation—doors and wooden windows recently scraped down and refinished, restored stone exterior, a small garden in front already prominently displaying well-disciplined clumps of hyacinths and daffodils.

"Quite cute," Dominique Larue said appreciatively, not without a mocking condescension of which he was ashamed.

"Yes," Gaby said, giving him a quick look.

"Does he live alone?"

"He lives there with a boy, quite young, his boyfriend I presume."

Again she glanced at him sideways, without questioning him. Her discretion, from the beginning, had been exemplary. Dominique had had only to demonstrate his helplessness—he wanted to find someone but all he knew was the first name and the profession he'd followed thirty years ago—and she had set herself in motion without telling him, spurred by the challenge or her friendship for him. Two days later, when he arrived at her place, she made him get in her car and drove him to Laval Street, and this trendily fixed up small house in front of which they were now parked like two private detectives on the trail.

"His last name is Gascon. He's forty-eight but looks a bit older. In exactly five minutes he will leave for work. He's been at the Ministry of Cultural Affairs for fifteen years. He bought the duplex in 1980, he rents the upper half to his sister Gisèle, divorced, who works as a municipal official. Every winter he goes to Guadeloupe for three weeks. Two years ago he almost died from a rare infection of the spleen, but he is now completely recovered. Would you like his social insurance number?"

"You're as good as the CIA," he said respectfully.

"Oh, I have contacts. And currently a lot of free time."

As always, she spoke with casual sarcasm, as though to make fun of herself, and for perhaps the first time Dominique was aware of her quiet charm. At the same time he had the feeling something was being wasted, this woman and he would not be getting to know each other better, yet he felt they shared many amazing similarities—including this strange habit she had, like him, of chewing her cheeks without realizing it whenever she felt the slightest degree of tension. Perhaps he could have loved her, now that was a ridiculous hypothesis, perhaps they could have had something together had it not been for the outsized shadow of Marie-Pierre, which obscured everything around her.

"Any news...of her?" he forced himself to ask coolly.

"No. She left all her things at my place, she's bound to come back for them. One day."

"One day," he repeated with a sad little laugh.

"Should I leave you here?"

"No doubt," sighed Dominique. "Thank you, thank you very very much."

Before getting out of the car he turned towards Gaby and they stayed there for an instant, in a ridiculous torpor, not knowing what to say. They almost kissed, but instead shook hands with ceremonious emotion, as though they both thought they'd never see each other again. Then Gaby's car disappeared around the corner of Pine, and Dominique, eyes narrowed to meet the rising sun, was left alone facing the house of Julien Gascon, the man who thirty years ago had stolen his father's love from him.

He didn't know how he would approach this man, what exact words could possibly be persuasive. What he did know was that he wanted this man to accompany him to see Maurice the following Thursday, he wanted to offer his father Julien Gascon, a beribboned gift that would say better than any lame words: look, I'm not judging you, you're not an ignominious old fag, look, Papa, I love you as you might have been. And then Maurice's eyes would overflow with emotion and surprise at the sight of little Julien returned, even for just a few hours; Julien Gascon would also have tears in his eyes, Dominique too, the whole thing, it went without saying, would be very melodramatic and very beautiful.

Given over to these streams of the future, Dominique almost missed the exit of a man who hurried out of the house, briefcase in hand, walking with the hurried step of someone who is late. Luckily the daffodils suddenly attracted his attention; the man with the briefcase slowed down, then squinted at the bulbs from every angle as though to search out some nasty little mite.

He was a heavyset man, just a very few ounces away from what would be called fat. He was wearing a light blue suit tight across the shoulders and bulging at the rear, which gave him the outdated silhouette of a lavender bottle, and he was reluctantly bald; that is, two or three grizzled locks of hair had been pitilessly drawn up from his neck, where they originated, to his smooth and chubby forehead—and this long journey had clearly not pleased them.

Dominique was greatly disappointed. Little Julien was not at all handsome. To be sure, the ravages of thirty years had accumulated, but how could he bring this bulging pastel jug to his father without it being taken as a huge mockery? Then he considered that Maurice himself was not exactly overburdened by beauty; at least this unplanned reunion might show them what each of them had escaped by breaking up in time.

Meanwhile, unconscious of the interest he had attracted, the man with the briefcase was humming as he searched through the daffodil leaves. Dominique came up to him.

"Julien Gascon?" he croaked.

The light blue suit made a quarter-turn, then Julien was facing him.

"That's me," he said, surprised.

Now, this was strange; the eyes of this greasy little Julien whoever looked at Dominique with a charming innocence. They were a very pure sea-blue that you might have stolen from some archangel, and you could suddenly see that bald little Julien might once have been handsome, in a sparkling way.

"My name is Dominique Larue."

"Larue, Larue...," he meditated, smiling. "That reminds me of something...."

Seeing the familiar sparkle of those eyes again, even just once might be enough to resurrect Maurice; and since Julien Gascon himself, despite thirty years' of decline, seemed to retain arcane memories, the meeting had to take place.

"Larue," he repeated, serious and contemplative. "Ah yes! LARUE! Aren't you the one who wrote *The Invisible Windowcleaner*? That must have been almost twelve years ago."

"Ah...uh...yes," Dominique agreed, totally stupefied.

"I knew it!" the other rejoiced, dropping his briefcase into the daffodils. "I never forget important names, and your novel was important, it gave one the feeling that something great was stirring, something that only had to mature to take flight. It was a terrific beginning—you haven't published anything since?"

"Well, actually..."

It had been so long since this had happened—since someone he didn't know had had something favourable to say about what he had written back then—so long since anyone but Mado had given him the feeling of being a real writer—that Dominique experienced an indescribable fear, immediately wiped away by delight.

"I'm just finishing something now," he strutted modestly. "I mean, it's finished, but I'm not entirely satisfied with the ending."

The beautiful eyes continued to contemplate the writer in him with a sincere deference that made Dominique want to hug him.

"A perfectionist, eh?" approved the sweet and charming Julien. "Twelve years to polish a novel and you don't think you're completely satisfied...oh, what a change from those diarrhoetics who inundate us with their first drafts every fall, so pitiful. And how did you get my name?"

"Get your name?" echoed Dominique, not seeing the connection.

"This program is still entirely confidential, but I can

guarantee you'll be admitted, and with a substantial bursary, we'll keep that between us, of course."

On these sibylline phrases the lower door of the duplex opened again, and into the daylight emerged a ravishing young man wearing a black sweatshirt and shorts so tight and short that on every second step a mischievous testicle tried to slip outside to see what was going on.

"Oh, Mathias!" Julien called, in a heavy Provençal accent.

"Oh, Julien!" Mathias returned in the same fashion—no doubt the two of them had just made their way through some Pagnolesque epic.

"Would you believe it? You know the new program I'm doing at the Ministry, 'Back to Creativity'? We haven't even printed the forms and writers are already coming to ask for grants."

"No," Dominique tried to correct him.

"What I think, honey," murmured the beautiful young man, "is that your briefcase is *squashing* the narcissus."

"Shit!" Julien exclaimed in a manly tone. "The neighbour's cat pissed on them again last night."

"No reason to *ass-ass-inate* them," replied the beautiful man in the titillating shorts, and off he jogged down Laval and disappeared more quickly than his shadow.

This led Julien to consider his schedule. He looked at his watch and yelped in panic.

"Come see me at my office," he said, swaying on the sidewalk. "'Back to Creativity' is meant to encourage dropouts from writing, it's just the thing for you. What's your novel about, exactly?"

"My God," Dominique responded, with a stab of pain at the involuntary evocation of Marie-Pierre's ghost. "It's about ... it's about sexual identity, I think."

"Sexual identity," Julien opined. "Very very good. Very exciting. It's time that a man interested himself in these things."

Dominique dared to bar his path, too bad for manners—and for the grant.

"Wait! You know my father," he let fly bluntly. "Maurice Larue. You had, you and he...when you worked at the Sagittarius Bookstore....It was thirty years ago....M-A-U-R-I-C-E L-A-R-U-E," he spelled fervently.

The blue eyes surveyed him with a flicker of impatience, then swivelled to the right, to the left, in search of times past.

"The Sagittarius Bookstore...yes, of course. I learned to read there, or almost. But you're taking me back to prehistory. Maurice Larue, you say?"

He smiled benevolently at Dominique, who seemed to be dying for his response.

"It's very possible," he said gently. "I knew so many, back then, you know how wild youth is....Come see me at my office," Maurice's one great love reiterated, trotting towards his Fuego. Dominique let him go forever: he really wasn't handsome, from behind, and, final consolation, his hair had just returned to its birthplace, leaving his head gleaming like a huge opal.

His mission aborted and the morning barely begun, Dominique resigned himself to going home. He had a home, after all, though these multiple peregrinations between the hospital Maurice had now left and the apartment that no longer contained Marie-Pierre had almost made him forget it. A home bejewelled by a loving little woman; what decent man would not find that fulfilling?

The door was open. Fear and trembling. How many robbers were sacking the interior? Did they have new weapons, were they eager to try them out? Serious riddles, those, which could have demanded that he go somewhere and lie down to reflect upon them, but Dominique, who had heroically advanced to the doorway, did not have the necessary time. A book hurtled towards him, soon imitated by works of varying weight and interest—among them he recognized his dictionary and his grammar, which whizzed by too quickly for him to greet them. Next, all his Bic pens leapt joyously forward, a kamikaze squadron resolved to poke his eyes out; then his portable Canon and a pretty desk lamp weighing fifty pounds or so crashed behind him; yet none of these familiar objects had ever shown a talent for flying.

Finally, at the other end of the corridor, he saw the loving little woman herself, Mado, the one who was trying to murder him with all these inanimate objects. Stupefaction.

"Liar!" She finally stopped, out of breath. "Bastard disgusting liar!"

She massaged her bicep for a moment, and looked into the whites of Dominique's eyes.

"I KNOW EVERYTHING!" she hammered out, her voice icy.

All right. If she said so. Dominique exhaled a long sigh, both exhausted and relieved of a substantial burden.

"How is Dr. Frolette?" Mado mocked. "Did he give you my money's worth? The couch in his office wasn't too uncomfortable?"

"It's true," Dominique instantly capitulated. "But I can pay you back right away for most of his—"

"THIEF!" Madeleine interrupted him. "Thief and

spineless creep! And you can't even stand up straight, even try to deny it. Pansy. DAMNED PANSY!"

That was upsetting. Now she too was starting to raise doubts about his inner identity—and in more incisive terms than Marie-Pierre.

"When I think," Mado kept on, "when I think that all the time you were pretending to have therapy on my money, you were having it on with....with a girl on the radio. What's she got that I haven't got? Look at her, a boring brunette, a timid little mouse..."

Suddenly Dominique noticed the photos; a whole section of the corridor wall was covered in blown-up images of Gaby, which Mado had been drumming with her fists the whole time she was talking.

"Gaby?" He was staggered. "No, you're totally mistaken!"

Mado howled. "And he denies it! He dares to deny it with the proof right in front of his eyes! There, look at yourself going back to her house, and look, here you are staring at each other like cats in heat! It's enough to make me sick! And this! And this!"

She began tearing up photos at random, including one taken that very morning, of Gaby's car, while they were watching the front of Julien Gascon's house.

"You see!" Mado cried triumphantly. "You can't say a word, can you? I hired a specialist to put all this together, a private detective, an expert in infidelity—and moreover he's Dr. Frolette's first cousin—HA!"

Family of incompetents, Dominique was thinking sadly, while congratulating himself on at least escaping the psychedelic sessions of the first. Then he asked himself if it was worth battling with his concubine to establish the real truth.

"You spent more time with her in six months than you spent with me in the past six years!"

"Listen," Dominique said. "That girl is just a friend who was letting someone stay at her house, someone who was a real inspiration for my novel—I only had a platonic relationship with…"

"SHUT UP!" Mado burst out. "If you're going to make things up, at least invent something less ridiculous!"

The most frustrating thing was that he couldn't even say Marie-Pierre's name, he was not allowed to invoke her precious existence, as though She had just been a fantasy. This was incredibly frustrating.

"I did not 'cheat' on you, as they say, with anyone else," he weakly reiterated, "but I admit the desire wasn't lacking."

"No," she ground out. "Probably what you were missing was the ability."

"The money for the clinic; I think I can pay you back the whole amount within, let's say….a month. Is that all right?"

In reply she gave a tense smile, then unfolded a piece of paper from her right hand.

"I've made a few calculations," she said, in a voice that was almost friendly. "Fifty-two weeks of supposed therapy at $50 each makes $2600, with current interest rates that comes to $2,912. I've been supporting you for two years, your accumulated share of the rent comes to $8,400, plus the utilities, $960, plus interest, $940: total—$10,300. Food and restaurants—$10,940—that's a very conservative estimate. Entertainment and travelling—$4,400. You borrowed the car a hundred and thirteen times—that's $2,260, and I'm not even counting the increases in the price of gas. In all, my love, you owe me $30,812," she finished with an acid laugh. "Do you think you can pay me that within a month?"

Dominique looked at her in shocked silence.

"The pain you have caused me can't be measured. You will leave this girl right away. There's no question of us separating, that would be too easy. I'll forget everything, even the money you owe me, on this sole condition: you give me your novel."

"My…"

"Your novel," she hissed, her eyes sparkling. "I want to put my name on it, to have it belong to me as though I had written it."

"You must be joking." Dominique burst out laughing.

"I am absolutely serious," Mado said.

She was. She was already going through the motions, very gracefully, of autographing copies.

TWENTY-THREE

TAKE a good look at them, Gaby. They say: I want. They have all sorts of ways of saying I want, subtly batting their eyes, an intimidating flash in their look, a peremptory tone of voice, sometimes fists, sometimes weapons—it depends on the program and the budget. It's the only way of getting things, women, the world: all those people who say I WANT, on television, are winners, Gaby. For years they've been telling you the rules of the game, clear and simple; how could you be passed by, poor shortsighted little girl, poor idiot, how could you misjudge the game for so long? And in addition to television series and dramas, there is the news, the interviews; look at them, Gaby, look at the people who influence events, people who are important, admire the way they're never caught with their guard down, how subtly they exude their warlike confidence; they lie so proudly it brings tears to our eyes, they betray with such conviction that we want to applaud them, they have mastered the art of appearing strong at all times, like mountains, like snakes. That's why they deserve to be who they are, President of the United States, Prime Minister of Canada, wealthy owners of mansions and factories. Women have been slower to play this game, it's true, but have no fear, they're catching up, they're gaining ground and winning battles, soon there will be no more sexism in the manly exercise of power.

Thus it was that Gaby let herself drift in the truth of the small screen, where the recipes for living are so generously prolific and available. The chips were positioned on her knees, her hand dipping into three open and almost empty bags so that she could mix flavours and types of grease, nestled at her feet was a majestic bottle of Pepsi-Cola that allowed her to hold off the desire for sleep. Because she had to stay up and prolong this significant day, the one on which, after a soporific gestation period of thirty-two years, the new Gaby had been born.

The new Gaby had been greeted obsequiously this morning by Mrs. Wagner in the CDKP foyer, an obsequious greeting she had kept herself from responding to, as befitted a distinguished on-air personality careful not to be too familiar with the masses. Because this new Gaby was a radio host—yes!—and officiated in the studio and time-slot previously reserved for Bob Mireau. Exit Bob Mireau, exit Priscilla-the-alluring. The revolution had been long and carefully planned; the former Gaby had wandered through life, her gums worn thin by insipid niceness, but this new Gaby had teeth.

Being strong and saying I WANT, first of all that meant knowing how to use the hidden sides of her fellow humans. For example, Henri-the-producer had no sense of humour and worshipped an image of himself that had nothing to do with reality, which comes to the same thing. So when one day he found on his desk a sixty-minute tape in which the spiritual voice of Bob Mireau declaimed elaborate jokes all of which more or less turned around him, his rounded belly, his horsy teeth and his bovine mind, Henri-the-producer was not at all pleased. Later, when the audience complaints began to flow into the studio, denouncing Bob Mireau's scandalous on-air drunkenness—which was somewhat annoying to CDKP's owner, who happened to be Henri's older brother and who blamed Henri—again Henri was not at all pleased. On the other hand, when Gaby, his former researcher, ended up in his bed without him doing anything to get her there, he who was in his disgraceful fifties, with a rounded belly and horsy teeth—that had pleased him, a lot without making him think there was a logical connection between these three events.

Of course, the recording—made during a wild party five years before—had been doctored by Gaby, the listeners' complaints about the apparent drunkenness of Bob Mireau all flowed from her loquacious pen and her multitalented voice, and the seduction of Henri, my God, had nothing to do with carnal desire.

Without suspecting anything, Henri-the-producer had innocently advanced the fatal pieces, check, while Gaby manipulated from afar. And so it happened that Bob Mireau was definitely a problem and then, unexpectedly, this Gaby presented an exciting idea for a new program—focussed on sexual perversions, what nectar to voyeuristic listeners— and after all, this little Gaby had a faultless voice and good diction and a knack for repartee and leadership and a radio personality's well-rounded soul and breasts, he had never noticed just how well rounded. Check and mate.

So simple, the rules of the game: any simple mind could decipher them. The problem was not with the rules but with the player, the one whose insides quivered with the (female?) fantasy of a world where all humans are brothers, all whales are protected, all blacks have souls, the Third Worlders have half our food and a sweet and sticky peace reigns throughout. And before making her first manly gesture, which would make a smooth passage for the others, Gaby had agonized like a mother giving birth to her first litter. Oscillating between horror and fascination, on the edge which would soon see her tumble down one side or the other, her Manichaeism painfully raw, she no longer ate or slept; she was in a state of collapse in this decisive battle that set her against herself. She had tried to explain what she was doing to Luc, when the sinister plan to shed Bob and attach herself to Henri began taking shape, she had wished, yes, with all her heart, that the one person in the world who said he loved her would intervene like a father in this silent battle—listen, she had wanted to say to him, I'm on the point of doing something irreparable, please stop me.

Luc had not been expecting her that evening, a Monday. She hadn't telephoned in advance, but he was quick to welcome her and invite her in; he had nothing and no one to hide.

"Make yourself at home," he suggested gently. "Put on some music, I'll just be a few minutes."

She followed him into the kitchen because she had come, really, in order not to spend one more second alone with the monster inside her.

Luc was cleaning the stove. All the elements had been taken off and were humbly steeping in cleaning solutions. From the oven, open like an oyster, the acrid stench of antibacterial hygiene. The parquet floor on which she posed a hesitant foot gleamed still water—and in fact it was still wet.

"GABY!" Luc cried. "I just waxed there!"

She stepped back, but too late.

"Shit, baby," he sighed more calmly, "I'm sorry, but just the same, when are you going to start looking where you're going?"

"Yes," Gaby stammered.

"It's like your hands, you're always sticking them all over the walls, look at the marks they leave...."

"Ah."

"Like a little kid," he teased her affectionately, "you're as messy as a little kid."

He grappled for a moment with the stove's enamel while Gaby contemplated the supple curvature of his back.

"Anyway," he said, turning around, "was there something particular you wanted?"

"Hmmm...," she began.

"SHIT!"

He suddenly flattened himself on the floor—catastrophe! A trickle of bleach was threatening to corrupt the beautiful wax, what a disaster!

Gaby left his place, and at the same time left part of her life, without him noticing. The last image she had of him was of a man genuflecting deeply on the floor, scraping and polishing like a despairing devotee.

Now, on the television, a woman was biting her lips and saying, "All this is driving me crazy," to a man who was sympathetically folding his arms around her, though in fact he was indifferent, you had to know how to read between the lines. Half an hour later the woman with the bitten lips was doubtless going to find out—at the same time as the idiotic viewer—that this man she had thought her own was keeping three mistresses and could no longer stand her smell. But Gaby would have foreseen the blow, oh no, she would never again be blinded by her own naivety.

Before turning on the television, she had put on the bird-shaped earring she had affectionately subtracted from

Marie-Pierre, and when she touched it inadvertently she thought she could see, suspended in front of her, the beautiful and impenetrable face of the transsexual.

"So?" Gaby demanded sharply. "Are you happy with me? Has my motive force expressed itself to your taste?"

But the features of Marie-Pierre, dulled by distance, were now replaced by the friendly cheerful face of Bob Mireau in the old days, and for a moment Gaby felt utterly overcome, thinking of the friendship and pure feelings that must still exist somewhere.

Was it her fault? After all, she had only defended herself. Was it her fault that life was like this, a fight to the finish in which a combatant who temporizes and weeps is a combatant defeated?

The new Gaby didn't weep, no longer knew how to weep. Dry-eyed, she watched the instructive little screen, all the while stuffing herself with chips, her powerful yang erect at her side.

TWENTY-FOUR

DOMINIQUE Larue was walking. It was summer and Sherbrooke Street glowed with mineral heat. Who ever said that Montreal was ugly and that concrete's baroque soul gave off no perfume? Dominique, happily breathing the city fumes, bounced as he strode, as though striding through prairie grass towards his true love.

With him he had the most essential of his earthly possessions, the two hundred and forty-six pages of his finished novel. Finished as much as anything ever can be, as finished as a grape or an airplane.

"I'd like to read what you're writing," Maurice had said, "I wouldn't mind having some idea of what you're doing." Dominique's heart had done a triple backwards somersault in his chest, then a jackknife-swallow dive. In his thirty-eight years of life he had never heard THAT in his father's voice, or anything more than polite curiosity or interest, like an evanescent spark of affection. Thus he ran to Maurice's, bringing him this offspring of the obscure zones of his brain, this strange grandson with its odd, perhaps harsh babble—but what did it matter? Their relationship would be transformed for good. Maurice would read the manuscript and it would hit him like an electric shock, because the truth was that Dominique had written it for Maurice, how could he not have realized that sooner—in order to bring together what was unconnected, in order to reach past Maurice's thorny silence, to stir in him the exploratory thoughts Marie-Pierre had sowed so densely in Dominique.

The only other copy had been mailed to Gaby, who would protect it, like a parent, against Mado's vengeful demands. Dominique had firmly resolved that she would never lay a hand on his work. Now was the time for decisive action; all that remained was deciding what to do.

Unexpectedly, he saw her on the other side of Sherbrooke Street, advancing like a lioness through the monolithic crowd, a large pink gabardine bag swinging airily against her shoulder. It was her. Finally. Marie-Pierre the questioner, the unique instigator of his fate—this he truly believed, and he was not mistaken, because it was while he was crossing the street to meet her that the Renault appeared. Small and plebian but resistant to the elements, the Renault crashed into him without surprising him; he felt no pain, to tell the truth, just a sudden weightlessness that relieved him of his body.

Others cried out in his place, esoteric faces above him filled with various emotions: "So you're still running away!" his mother scolded, her small disciplined chignon in place and her pearl scarf around her neck the way it had been in her grave fifteen years ago; a cat he had once loved that had been taken by leukemia came to lick his chin; several sunsets traced their orbits over Mount Athos, to which he found himself transported, and from his left side he saw emerging a small timorous boy, an old man who walked erectly and had no face, a graceful young woman who resembled him in all ways, a yellow mare with an old lady's face, and he thought these were all pieces of himself he'd kept prisoner inside, now breaking away and leaving, and suddenly he missed the perniciousness of life's hopes, even the futile ones, the smell of warm bread and the voices of the women he would never meet, but then he was surrounded by a light that silenced his anguish and convinced him that he was finally free, and then he didn't miss anything anymore, because he was dead.

Unaware of the metallic noises behind it, the pink gabardine bag continued on its way and disappeared, and Dominique Larue's two hundred and forty-six pages were sent swirling into the air, overtaken by a travelling frenzy that scattered them all over the city of Montreal.

Page 236 came to rest at the heel of Bob Mireau, moored to the terrace of the Café Cherrier; in Lafontaine Park, where he was feverishly pacing, Lucky Poitras almost stepped on page 214; Michèle saw page 46 fly through the window of her law office on Rue Saint-Jacques and thought the city was becoming decidedly unhealthy; J. Boulet berated a student who had made a paper airplane with page 37 and sent it into Mme Trotta's face; page 173 was discovered by Luc on his apartment balcony, and he put it right in the wastebasket; a female squirrel on Mount Royal lined her nest with page 118 and there gave birth to five offspring in excellent health.

So insignificant, human life and death, Camille was thinking that very night under the pale summer-solstice sky: microbe acrobatics, flickers lost in thundering space. Deneb, for example, would still be alive in 15 million years, whereas mere men, who struggled for half a century at best, wasted their minuscule turn in the sun sleeping, eating poisoned things and buying shoes.

Contemplating Deneb and the cross of the Swan lying in

the midst of the Milky Way gave Camille the feeling she was in secret communication with her father. Because that was the constellation on the cherished postcard he had sent her three months earlier, which she had carried with her ever since, a ragged talisman.

She had always liked the Swan, which harbours so many splendours in so few stars: at the tip of the main arm, majestically begun by Deneb, there was—among others—Albireo, very sober in appearance, which the telescope revealed to be magically double, half gold, half sapphire; at the feet of Albireo was the miniconstellation of the Arrow, which sketched a comical hydroplane invisible to the naked eye; and of course there was the nebulous America, trying to conceal its triangular silhouette to Deneb's left; and near Epsilon was the beautiful dim lace of the Swan, final residue of a fat star that had exploded at the dawn of the human age, perhaps some Cro-Magnon had spotted it in its supernova phase, how would anyone ever know?

And Camille, as she adjusted the eyepiece of her telescope for NGC 6960, marvelled at the fact that time meant so little, Deneb's light took millions of years to reach her while just a few brief moments separated her from adulthood, but God how those few brief moments seemed an eternity....

As she put her eye to the telescope, something suddenly obstructed her view—a satellite, no doubt, which wasn't moving on and would soon fill her whole field of vision with its chalky light. She pulled back her head, gradually taken over by a fantastic exhilaration, a fever that made her bones go soft: it wasn't a satellite. It was huge and very bright, it overflowed the telescope now, it was consuming a larger and larger portion of the sky and was coming slowly towards this place, towards me, Camille thought, moving back, moving back, until her motion was vetoed by the rough bark of a tree trunk. A supernova, she stammered to herself, suddenly knowing that it was none of those things, neither a supernova nor any knowable object, words were useless to designate whatever was approaching her and wasn't a star, because slowly the light was dimming and the object took on defined and elongated contours, like a rib inflated at one end, then came to a stop a hundred meters away, quietly resting on the line of the horizon.

She had to run, whatever had arrived was not meant for human eyes, but despite herself Camille was frozen against the bark of the tree. The tip of the object had taken on an incandescent clarity, and something emerged from it and began advancing towards her, slender and phosphorescent, like a moving column of energy, and Camille realized that it was alive. This is happening to me, it's happening to ME, she told herself in magical terror, and the weakly glowing thing stopped in front of her, stopped in an incredible silence, she must speak and demand the answer to the great mysteries where it came from how and why death life the beginning of the stars—"What…what sex are you?" Camille articulated weakly, and the thing held out something like a light towards her, which seemed to warm her belly, and then suddenly there was nothing, no longer anything but the smell of scorched grass and an arrow of light vanishing into the sky.

Camille collapsed on the ground. She was crying and laughing at the same time and then, tickled by a sudden moisture, she touched herself and discovered that blood was flowing out between her legs.

TWENTY-FIVE

ABY heard about Dominique Larue's death on the television news. The same day, she had received his manuscript in the mail. It was very badly typed and on the title page he had simply noted, a premonitory wink, "Everything, happily, comes to an end."

She looked over the last lines: "She had already moved on, she was walking alone and triumphant, trailing her ethereal scent, she was on her way to another place to disturb the infallible and the righteous-minded."

So it was true, he had been able to finish it, this painful necessity that had set him buzzing around Marie-Pierre like a terror-stricken wasp. And since she had truly liked Dominique Larue, and hadn't had time to tell him so, Gaby felt the irresistible need to take something from him, this last and unique vestige that had been left behind; she signed the manuscript with her name and, crossing her fingers, took it to a publisher.

She would become an astrophysicist. Later a magnificent tower would be erected at the summit of some mountain, and she would live there with her father, once again celebrated and respected. They would tame eagles, they would lose themselves in their respective passions, fluttering from discovery to discovery. And people would come from all over to consult them and offer them awards, but they would make fun of them and send the eagles to peck at their bums.

Later. But while she waited it was necessary to go through the necessary changes, to become a woman. And Camille, with no preliminary gropings, installed the first tampon of her life. Michèle, who saw her as she passed by the open door, cried out in fright.

"Oh my dear girl," she said, upset, when Camille came out of the bathroom, "you didn't tell me, you're a big girl now...."

She tried to embrace Camille, who slipped out of her arms.

"Do you want to talk about it a bit?... Should we discuss ... it?"

"There's no point," Camille said coldly, "I know everything there is to know about women and men."

Michèle's face darkened; she continued to stare at her daughter with a smile that tried not to tremble.

"A boy phoned for you a little while ago," she continued in a low voice. "Lucky something...."

"Oh?" Camille said, not surprised, a fleeting light in her eyes. "He'll probably call back..."

She started towards her room but Michèle grasped her shoulder.

"Please, Camille," she said humbly. "Please." Her face looked as worn as a grandmother's, and suddenly Camille saw her as she really was, a fragile human being doing her best to salvage a few crumbs of happiness from her life. "I'm going to leave him," Michèle said. "I'm breaking up with J. Boulet."

Camille tapped her arm with all the friendship she was capable of—how foreign her skin seemed.

"No," she said gently. "Get married. Marry him, I mean it. I'll be the maid of honour if you like."

Dumbfounded, Michèle sought sarcasm in her voice, but there was none. She watched her daughter moving off with the stride of a nymph—grown tall and incomprehensible—a kind of aura seemed to be carrying her away, she was leaving and she was untouchable, no one would ever be able to hurt her again.

TWENTY-SIX

SHE was going away. A pink gabardine bag, new and ready to welcome the world, like her, was bouncing against her shoulder, she was going empty-handed so that lightness would not be lacking in the exciting life that awaited her.

The youngest power on earth had been titillated by her *curriculum vitae* and her perverse status of intelligent transsexual, three job offers had arrived simultaneously from California—a post as researcher at the Science Institute, a professorial chair at UCLA, a job as a television hostess on NBC. Marie-Pierre had accepted them all because, since she had conquered her inner demons, she had been breathing out whirlwinds of energy. The vane of madness had departed, leaving her fresh and powerful, it was like the first day of the resurrection.

The airport, shiny and air-conditioned, bustled in the midst of the great undaunted birds. Marie-Pierre watched the men and women, dazed by the future, hurrying towards the counters, and she told herself that they all carried their secret duality within them: here a woman was laughing in the voice of that man, there a man was musing beneath the makeup of that woman, each of them was two, and trying so hard to be unshakably one. Someday she would tell them, someone should tell them.

Quickly she cut through them—that caused a break in the rectilinear perfection of the lineup, but then everything became smooth and monochrome again. She had already moved on, she was walking alone and triumphant, trailing her ethereal scent, she was on her way to another place to disturb the infallible and the righteous-minded.

Ville de Montréal

Feuillet
de circulation

À rendre le		
Z 1 1 JUIN 1997		
Z 0 1 AOU 1997		
Z 1 1 OCT 1997		

06.03.375-8 (05-93)